MURDER FOR MONEY

It was a distastefully routine case for Detective Sam Adams when a derelict human being known as Sauerkraut was murdered — until a sinister overtone involving narcotics became evident. After that, it became a case with fascinating sidelines. One of them was the ingenious manner in which the heroin was smuggled into the US. Another was that the stateside leader of the smugglers was also wanted for espionage. Finally Sam Adams, with Detective Lieutenant Stokes, set a trap for the criminals . . .

HUNTER LIGGETT

MURDER FOR MONEY

Complete and Unabridged

LINFORD
Leicester

First published in Great Britain in 1969 by
Robert Hale & Company
London

First Linford Edition
published 2000
by arrangement with
Robert Hale Limited
London

British Library CIP Data

Liggett, Hunter, *1916* –
    Murder for money.—Large print ed.—
Linford mystery library
1. Detective and mystery stories
2. Large type books
I. Title
823.9'14 [F]

ISBN 0–7089–5740–4

Published by
F. A. Thorpe (Publishing)
Anstey, Leicestershire

Set by Words & Graphics Ltd.
Anstey, Leicestershire
Printed and bound in Great Britain by
T. J. International Ltd., Padstow, Cornwall

This book is printed on acid-free paper

1

Bases for Murder

Sam Adams was one of those powerfully built, seemingly imperturbable and pragmatic people who spoke only when he had something to say, and whose words fell with the weight of solemn pronouncements, as now, when he looked at his secretary on the third floor of police headquarters at Manhattan's detective bureau, Fourth Precinct, and said, 'There are only two causes of murder, Helen. money and passion. I've been a cop eighteen years, a detective ten, and on that kind of experience I put money far ahead of passion.'

Helen had intensely blue eyes, short-cut taffy hair that she wore lightly curled, and although no one would ever have had the *chutzpa* to mistake Helen Moran for a boy, she somehow got that impression across; a boyish-girl.

1

She couldn't have weighed more than a hundred and fifteen pounds, if that much, to Sam Adams' two hundred pounds, and her five feet and three inches left her a head shorter as well. Furthermore, her definitely Saxon look contrasted with what could have been Black-Irish hair, brows and eyes, in Sam Adams, although it could just as easily have been that Sam had an Italian grandfather.

There was one other thing; Sam had become a uniformed patrolman right out of the army, where he'd lied about his age, but he'd been in policework as he'd said, eighteen years, and he was now thirty-seven years of age to Helen's twenty-four. It wasn't an unpardonable gap; it wasn't even a very unusual one providing a woman of twenty-four preferred the company of men in their late thirties, but in the view of younger policemen who had occasion from time to time to visit the office of Sam Adams, it was a crying shame that Helen was so patently and cheerfully gone on 'old' Sam Adams.

If he'd been married it would have

been a cause of great glee too, but he wasn't; had never been married in fact.

The result of his personal invulnerability surrounding exciting little Helen Moran, was elemental; she barely even saw the younger policemen, and when Sam Adams had a troublesome case, she lived every breath of it right alongside him.

Now, perched on the edge of his desk in the little private office directly behind her own outer office, she listened to brooding Sam Adams as though he were the original Oracle of Delphi, or at the very least, an ordained preacher of the True Gospel.

'But, you see, it's not always simple deciding which it is, money or passion, although once that *is* determined, then a detective is faced with a good deal of patient leg work. By process of elimination, he usually can make a decent arrest.'

Helen, having worked for Sam for four years now, having typed all his reports, his expense-accounts, even his personal depositions and those of criminals and suspects he'd brought in when asked

3

by him to do so, knew what he was now saying was the absolute truth. She also knew, knowing Sam, that there was more to come, for he had only that very morning been handed a new assignment, and *that* was the horned dilemma.

'But suppose you come upon a murder where there is no money *or* passion involved?'

She smiled, saying nothing. Her figure was firm and handsome, perched there on the side of the desk. She also knew that.

Sam wasn't looking at her. His attention was glued to a glossy eight-by-ten photographic print showing a rumpled human body, face up. The corpse was male, emaciated, perhaps fifty years of age, wearing thread-bare tropical worsteds, once white, now a uniform dirty grey, without socks on the feet, or a hat or a tie. Altogether, even alive, the man would have been unpleasant, but dead he was much more, he was sickening.

There was a bullet-hole in the precise centre of the soiled forehead, nearly

4

obscured by great shocks of lank, black hair.

Helen, avoiding that photograph with a vengeance, said, 'Passion, Sam. If he had no money, access to none, then it had to be passion, didn't it?'

'Look at him, Helen.'

'I did and no thank you, not again. Anyway, just because he was a derelict lacking visible means of support doesn't mean he couldn't have aroused some homicidal maniac, does it?'

Sam raised his dark, doe-like eyes. 'Homicidal maniacs, even the ones who avoid personal contact with victims, don't pump one bullet into a man's brain then turn and walk away. They shoot again and again. They kick a victim, strike him, slash and scratch and go all to pieces. There's nothing easier than running down a murder-maniac.'

Sam leaned and placed two huge hands palms-down on either side of the glossy photograph. 'What other kind of passion?'

Helen wouldn't look around and down. 'Vengeance?'

5

'Possibly. What else?'

'Sam, it's almost five o'clock.'

'Okay. Go on home.'

'I wasn't thinking like that, Sam, I was thinking you have that meeting at seven, upstairs.'

Without removing his eyes from the picture Sam grunted. 'Meetings aren't important. I'll be there on time, don't worry. What other kind of passion, Helen?'

'A woman; a torrid affair with a married woman?'

'Oh for the lord's sake, Helen. This man was a total alcoholic. He was living on borrowed time. He couldn't have felt anything for the most beautiful woman on earth. No. It's something else.'

'All right. *You* tell *me*.'

Sam threw himself back in the swivel-chair. 'I don't know. Money or passion, and by gawd here's one that doesn't fit either category.'

Helen got off the desk, glanced at her watch and went as far as the door before speaking again. 'You know perfectly well it's got to be one or the other.'

Sam looked steadily at her before speaking, then smiled. 'Not money, Curly-head. If it's passion it's some variety that'll have to crop up to be recognized, because as of right now I'm helpless.'

'What about the identification?'

'That's all being fed through the IBM machines downstairs. The bird's whole history.'

'There's nothing you can do until you have some help, Sam, so why don't you go home and rest for a couple of hours before the meeting upstairs?'

He yawned mightily without bothering to drop a hand over his mouth. 'I'd just get home and have to turn right around and drive back. I'll close my eyes right here for forty winks. Good night, Curly-head.'

She smiled, walked out, closed the door and stood a moment on the far side of it debating about going downstairs to get a glass of milk and a ham sandwich on rye — Sam Adams's favourite. She decided, for some perverse reason known only to herself, not to do it, grabbed her

7

coat, hat, handbag and gloves, flipped the cover over her typewriter and hiked on out into the lighted cement corridor.

The detective bureaux always had reminded her of the dungeon of some musty old castle. It didn't help much to ask the maintenance people to use lysol in their scrub-water when they swabbed down the floor and walls; that only made the dungeon smell like a leprosarium; at least her *idea* of what a leprosarium smelled like.

Sam, back there at his desk like a massive Buddha, hunched round that disgusting police photograph of death even went with the unpleasant image Helen Moran had of the place where she worked.

Except of course that she understood Sam; he wasn't really as forbidding as he looked at all. He was gentle and considerate, sweet and thoughtful.

She met a girl named Margery Fein who worked for Detective Lieutenant Richard Stokes — called 'Old Ironsides' behind his back — at the lift, and in response to Margery's enquiry, Helen said her boss was still working, that he'd developed a habit of doing that over the years that nothing seemed able to break.

Margery Fein was a dark, un-pretty girl noted especially round the second floor for a phenomenal memory and legs like a sparrow, and she too, was single. But *her* boss, Lieutenant Stokes was in his mid-fifties, married and with three grandchildren, so, while Margery kept a hopeful eye peeled, she also took vicarious interest in Helen's romance with Sam Adams.

Now, she said, 'Look, Helen, you've got to jar that big bear out of his rut. You've got to . . . have you ever suggested the Boardwalk on Sunday, or maybe the beach? You'd look perfect in one of those Italian bikinis.'

'I wouldn't *feel* so perfect,' muttered Helen, as the automatic lift dumbly opened for them.

'Moonlight car-riding then,' persisted Margery, and rolled her eyes exasperatedly. 'How long does it go on like this?'

'He's taken me out, Marge.'

'I can guess. Over dinner he's wondering who disemboweled some wino on skid-row. A romance like that shouldn't happen to your worst enemy. Honey, it's up to you.'

Helen smiled as the lift lurched to a shuddering halt on the ground floor. 'I know it is, and I'll work it out. My horoscope in the newspaper says this isn't actually a very good year for people under my sign to get married, Marge.'

They parted at the doorway leading to the street beyond. Margery rode with three other girls who were also employed in the building. Helen had her own car — a rather silly luxury, actually. People living in down-town Manhattan needed cars like Custer needed more Indians. Still, Helen had a very strong maternal instinct; she loved to care for things. A husband would have been ideal. But she didn't have a husband, she had a car.

There were store-lights on, multi-coloured, although because it was early summer the sun hadn't gone out of the sky yet. It just had stopped brightening anything lower than the fifty-fifth floor, which meant the cement canyons were already full of dusk.

Helen drove the fourteen blocks to her hotel — strictly for the working woman, a sign said inside the tiny lobby — left her car parked out back and rode another lift, this time up instead of down.

Her apartment was actually one rather large room with two flimsy partitions, but it was home, it was private, and everything in it except the plumbing and tiny stove belonged to her.

It also had a window overlooking the maze below. If the view never did inspire her very much, at least the window upon occasion, when the sky was clear once or twice a year, could be opened to admit air. For the other three hundred and sixty-three days of the year it remained closed, bolted, unwashed on the outside, and useful only as a means for seeing the Brooks Brothers Clothing Store's giant clock across the way and down below.

In Manhattan windows had long since ceased to have an aesthetic function.

11

Unless they were used to display something for sale, clothing, bedding, pastrami, gefelte-fish, they could only serve some such function as the one for which Helen used her window.

2

Sauerkraut

Sam had the identification of that emaciated corpse, finally. It did not, as he pointed out to Helen the morning after he'd got the assignment, give him any very helpful suggestions, but then identifications seldom were solutions in themselves. On the favourable side, however, once someone in whom the law was interested was identified, the first giant step could be taken.

Sam said, 'Now we back-track, find relatives, friends, creditors, enemies, and eventually a motive for murder — then a murderer.'

'Who was he, Sam?' asked Helen, very appealing this morning in a blue blouse that matched her eyes and a beige skirt darker than her hair.

Sam lit up, blew smoke at the ceiling and gazed without concerted interest at the paper in his hand. 'Franz Ludwig. No felony record, although he has a background of misdemeanours going back many years, and he has also been listed as a Missing Person at least once a year for the past ten.'

'Married, Sam?'

'Single man. Thirty-four years of age — '

'Thirty-four! Sam, in that picture he looked closer to sixty.'

'He's been an alcoholic for ten years according to the record, Helen, which means he was probably a hard drinker for five years before that. His kind age rapidly. I've seen them so debilitated they look seventy when they're half as old. Anyway, Franz Ludwig was thirty-four, single, college-educated — which doesn't guarantee much, although as a rule *that* kind doesn't hit skid-row until they are older — and believe it or not, Mister Ludwig was at one time considered likely to become a master concert pianist.'

Helen leaned her chin on one palm and gazed at big Sam, sitting beside her desk in the outer office. 'How awfully tragic,' she murmured. 'I suppose he had a mother.'

'Well, no one's discovered a way to synthesise 'em yet. As a matter of fact his parents are still around. They had two other children, a son and a daughter, both married. The parents and the others are law-abiding people, no trouble, moderately well-off.' Sam punched out the cigarette in Helen's onyx ashtray — kept on her desk for visitors since she did not smoke — 'And now we come to the murder.'

Helen brightened. 'Money or passion, Sam?'

A fleeting spasm of pain shadowed his features then was gone. 'Who knows?'

'What does that mean?'

'So far, Helen, all we have is his name and the fact that he was a confirmed lush. That doesn't add up to a whole lot. I'd guess there must be a hundred thousand alcoholics between New York City and Manhattan Island. I've got to start the leg-work today: See his parents, his brother and sister, dig up his friends, if he had any, do the background spadework.' Sam yawned, this time behind his hand, and gloomily gazed at the paper in his other hand. 'I wonder how many of these derelicts turn up every couple of days in alleys, door-ways, under the docks, and get dumped in Potter's Field without any fuss? Probably hundreds, but this one has to get shot so I end up with him.'

'You don't sound very sympathetic, Sam.'

He looked up at her. 'Sympathetic? Curly-head, I'm not sorry for the *other* ones, how could I feel sorry for one like this? Thirty-four, comfortable background, talent, and he throws all of it away for booze. Sympathetic? I'm disgusted.'

Sam rose and went out the office door, forgetting his hat which wasn't unusual. He had already arranged with the Transport Pool for the car that was waiting out front, and as soon as he'd slid behind the wheel he could have closed his mind and proceeded on instinct. He'd gone through this identical routine hundreds of times. He had the address

16

of the dead man's parents, which was his first stop. From there he'd go and see the brother, the sister, glean a few other names, visit other homes, other stores, finally, the skid-row gin-mills and dockside alleyways. The only thing that made Franz Ludwig's passing a police undertaking was that little puckered hole in Ludwig's forehead.

He could even have predicted the distress of the parents, the anguish of the brother and sister, the blank impassivity of the bartenders along skid-row where other ambulatory scarecrows stirred uneasily at sight of Sam's I.D. folder and badge.

Up to a point every bit of it was routine, even the tears. They came on cue, as did the head-shakes of the barmen who couldn't remember anyone named Franz Ludwig even by description, but somewhere along the route a subtle change occurred; somewhere between the residence of Franz Ludwig's relatives and the dives he'd frequented prior to his passing, anguish became blankness, outcries became strong silence, and all

Sam got was wet and uncomfortable stares.

This was where he had to come to life. Leaving the clean, orderly world of the relatives, Sam went down into that other world with every sense alert because along here some place he would find a hint or a revelation that would take him along to wherever Franz Ludwig had gone in search of his private ending.

But Sam Adams did not expect help from the other derelicts or the gin-mill proprietors who lived off the derelicts. He had a much more reliable source of information: the policemen who patrolled skid-row.

Ordinarily they were grey and grizzled — and disillusioned — harness-bulls, or else they were suffering novices whose sensitivities were being cruelly blunted by a tour of duty in an area that every fledgling patrolman had to serve in at least for a while.

They knew their beats and their charges. They referred to their people by the names the derelicts had acquired in their own sordid environment. The name

18

Franz Ludwig, for instance, turned out to mean nothing at all, but the designation Sauerkraut had significance.

'Harmless,' the patrolman told Sam Adams. 'He used to be a periodic; showed up down here maybe once a year. Then twice a year. You know the route. We'd get a Missing Persons report, pick him up, haul him in, and maybe for a couple of months he wouldn't be around. Then, there he is again, perched on a bar-stool. After a time no more Missing Persons reports.'

'Friends?' asked Sam.

The patrolman looked at his partner as though to imply that every time a derelict got his personal Deep Six, people asked the same silly questions.

'They don't have friends. They live in tribes. You know? Like this: Maybe three or four of them bum around together. Maybe it's six or seven of them. Never more than six or seven though. They do that for protection; always some other one thinks he can beat up a guy and rob him. They're all too far gone to put up much of a scrap, so they gang-up into little tribes.

It's not a matter of friendship. If you went right now and asked Sauerkraut's tribe what happened to him, they probably couldn't even remember the guy. Ask the medics, they'll tell you these loonies don't have functioning memories any more. And when one disappears there's always another one to take his place. No one remembers the others, like your man Ludwig.'

Sam was polite. 'You could write a book.'

'Yeah? And who'd read it? Who gives a damn?'

'You're probably half right. But if Ludwig's associates wouldn't remember him, someone would. Someone shot him in the head.'

The patrolman said, 'I know that. I'm the guy who turned it in. My partner and I found him.'

'Where?'

'It's in the report I filed. In an old warehouse down on the dock lying on his back in a nest of old newspapers and empty bottles. We find them like that every day or so.'

20

'With bullet-holes in them?'

'No,' conceded the patrolman. 'That part was unusual. But none of the rest of it was.'

'About that bullet-hole: Do you find arms on them, as a rule?'

The patrolman made an ugly little laugh. 'You don't find *anything* on them, usually. When they get down here they've pawned wristwatches, rings, even partial dentures and spectacles. I can't remember when I found one carrying a gun.'

'Or with a hand steady enough to aim and fire it?'

'Or with enough left inside his skull to motivate him to do any such thing, Mister Adams. They're like wraiths — like smelly ghosts. They can't concentrate for more than a minute or two at a time. They jerk around like tin monkeys on a string. They burst into tears for no reason and they jump up swatting at imaginary mosquitoes without any warning.'

'But *someone* had a steady hand and a motivated mind; maybe he wasn't one of them.'

'Probably not. But we very rarely see

21

any other kind down here. And as far as Sauerkraut was concerned, he was one of the typically harmless, swiftly degenerating ones. My partner and I've discussed it; neither of us have ever seen him in the company of anything but his own kind. We've asked around.' The patrolmen lifted big shoulders and let them fall. 'Nothing.'

Sam said, 'I'm not really too much concerned with who shot him, but I'd give a lot to know *why*. Tell me, do you have addicts down here, pushers; how about muggers and petty thieves?'

'Mister Adams, these bums have nothing worth stealing. As for pushers, our people are too far gone on booze — wine usually when they get as far as Sauerkraut — to react to dope. But most important of all, they don't have money enough for pushers to be interested in them.'

'What *do* they have that would interest felons?'

'That's just it — nothing. Hell; they can't even be recruited to run simple errands, because one minute after they are told to do something, they forget it

22

entirely.' The patrolman regarded Sam Adams with a little pity. 'I know what you're up against and I wish I could help you, but it's just a blank. Why not slip it into the U-file and forget it. There sure as hell are more solution-oriented murders on the books. And Sauerkraut was a total nobody. Go and ask at the dump where he got his wine every day and they wouldn't even remember him. He was a skinny, dirty, faceless nobody. The tax-payer's money should be spent on guys like him getting hit? Look, if you want another way to look at it, Sauerkraut was a lot better off dead than alive.'

Sam said, 'You're sure of that are you?'

The patrolman spread his hands. 'He sure as hell had nothing going for him *alive*. I'm sure of *that*.'

Sam decided to go look at the warehouse, got directions and left the patrolmen to their unlovely assignment.

The neighbourhood along the docks was windy, filthy, smelly and uncompromisingly ugly. The warehouse itself had a red placard nailed to a rotting door saying it had been condemned by the city's Building and Safety Department.

It obviously hadn't been used in years although it *had* been inhabited. Sam saw one of the inhabitants a moment after he stepped inside the foetid-smelling place; a wharf-rat as large as a small cat.

Otherwise, though, there wasn't any life stirring.

He found the place where Franz Ludwig had died. There still remained a chalk outline on the floor where the body had been. Nearby were the crates, bottles, filthy rags, rumpled newspapers where men had hunched together in deranged despair. It was not an atmosphere Sam Adams hadn't encountered before but that didn't make it pleasant now.

Light came through a rotting old roof but where Ludwig's 'tribe' had congregated it was dark, as though the derelicts shunned brightness — which they did, although not as sociologists professed, because they instinctively sought womb-gloom — but because bright light hurt their constantly watering eyes.

Sam sought diligently for the bullet-mark in the rotting planks, found it, found that someone had pried the lead out, and because that's all he had for his day's work, decided to go back to the ballistics laboratory and see what had been turned up about the slug that had deprived Franz Ludwig of his wasted and worthless life.

The stench of dockside lingered long after Sam was back in the different-smelling but equally as odorous business section of the city. The memory of wasted bodies and grey faces remained with him also. Regardless of how tough and sanguine an eighteen-year-veteran of police work was, he had values, principles, senses, just like other people. Total human degradation, accustomed or not, marked him each time he saw it and moved through it.

By the time Sam reached the laboratory he couldn't have smiled if his life had depended upon it.

3

A Beginning

'You're sure? It couldn't have just got misplaced, or perhaps lost in transit?'

The laboratory technician, a youngish man with jet-black hair and eyes, a definitely Sephardic look, said, 'Look; if the bullet had been sent in, we'd have it, Mister Adams. They don't get lost or misplaced. We got a receiving routine that's absolutely foolproof. If anyone had filed a report with us, we'd have that too. If there'd been a bullet *or* a report, one or the other of them would be here. I been in the lab six years and I've never once seen any evidence lost. Not once. I'll tell you what I think, Mister Adams; that bullet wasn't dug out of the floor by a cop.'

Sam returned to his office just as Helen was putting the plastic cover over her typewriter. She beamed him a wonderful smile, the first of its kind he'd seen all day.

'Well . . . ?' she threw out at him, eyes alight with expectation.

He saw his hat on the wall-rack, remembered forgetting it, went and straddled the chair beside her desk and fished for the rumpled packet of cigarettes to light one before he spoke.

'There's no bullet. Someone pried it out of the planks where Ludwig was killed, but it wasn't turned into the lab. And there's no reason for Ludwig to have been shot.'

Helen thumbed through some papers in a wooden mail-basket, selected one and offered it as she said, 'You are so right, Sam. If someone had only waited a little while longer they wouldn't have had to shoot Mister Ludwig, he'd have died unassisted. This is the Coroner's report.'

Sam nodded, took the paper but didn't look at it. 'So why *didn't* someone wait?'

Helen's eyes, as blue as new corn-flowers, remained steadily pleasant as she said, 'I haven't the foggiest, Sam.'

'Neither have I,' he confessed, stuffing the Coroner's report into a side-pocket.

'You're surely not stumped.'

He regarded her stonily. 'What would be so terrible about that?'

'Nothing,' she replied, reaching to pat one huge paw where it lay on her desk. 'Only you aren't. I know you too well for that. You've got *something*.'

He nodded very gently. 'What I've got I'd trade for an old gold tooth highly polished. Curly-head, Ludwig was a nothing. Not just a bum, not just a degraded human being, he was a total nothing. They don't even remember what he looked like down there where he's been spending all his life. And he's only been dead two days.'

'What about his other contacts, Sam?'

'Nice Jewish family. Mama is fat and sat wringing her hands and sobbing. Papa is a little less fat and sat slightly rocking back and forth like he might be saying a silent chant of some kind. The sister and brother were different. Sister cried and wanted to know what kind of a God would let such talent end up on a refuse pile. Brother was resentful, bitter, and understandably relieved. He said they'd all been putting in a little each month for Franz, and he couldn't have afforded it much longer, what with his family coming on and all.'

'That all sounds normal, Sam.'

'Very normal. I suppose it's even normal that Ludwig's cronies down under the docks in that stinking old warehouse don't remember, two days later, that he ever existed. Improbable but normal, at least down there. Curly-head, what *isn't* normal is that someone would bother to hit this derelict at all.'

'Sam, but someone *did* hit him.'

'Okay. Now tell me why?'

'I can't.'

'Neither can I — yet. But I'll tell you one thing: The only thing Ludwig had going for him was total anonymity. No one knew him, no one remembered him, no one cared a damn about him and he was thoroughly expendable. *That's* the only thing he had of any value.'

'Sam . . . ?'

'Wait a minute, Helen. There are thousands upon thousands of people who wish they could become as thoroughly forgotten as Ludwig. There are probably even more people who could use a person like that — someone no one knows or would remember. And of course the beauty of using someone like Sauerkraut, you see, is that like a disposable dishrag, afterwards he simply disappears. Goes down under the docks, or into some abandoned warehouse, and quietly dies.'

'Only he didn't.'

'Curly-head, that's right. Only Ludwig had the nerve to linger on and on. He wouldn't oblige. The Coroner may say he'd have died within another month or two, and probably that's right. Only someone else wanted him to pass on sooner — right away — and this he wouldn't do.'

'Sam, where do you go from here?'

Adams raised an oaken wrist for a silent moment then lowered it. 'Home to shower, shave and change, then out to dinner.'

'Alone, Sam?'

He looked at her, blinked several times then said, 'No. Not necessarily alone. We could go together.'

Helen sprang up, plucked her coat from the wall-rack and said, 'Give me an hour.' She bent, pecked him on the cheek and fled out of the office. He put out his cigarette, leaned back on the wall and considered the door. Aloud, he repeated what she'd said.

'Sam, where do you go from here?'

Then he arose, put the chair where it belonged, beside the desk, got his hat and also walked out of the office. He knew *exactly* where he went from here.

Later, freshly dressed, as though leaving his other clothes also meant leaving behind that seamy segment of existence he'd journeyed through earlier in the day, he felt better. By the time he got to Helen's place he could even smile a little.

This was the other Sam Adams, not startlingly different, of course, but different.

They had two restaurants they preferred. Manhattan was a place where dining out had ceased to be a ritual long before, but it also was a place where every foreigner could find a national eatery. Sam and Helen, with whatever latent affinities subconsciously lingered, liked an English inn-type restaurant, and a Hungarian goulash palace. The latter, through some lofty, although seemingly inconsistently bizarre rationalization of its owner, existed in the heartland of a solid Jewish neighbourhood.

Tonight they went to the English restaurant whose simulated age-darkened walls, beamed ceiling and subdued air of imperturbable antiquity suited Sam's mood. Barely had their roast beef arrived than Sam said, 'Now tell me, Helen, what kind of person would use a man like Ludwig?'

She was accustomed to his feat of total recall and cerebral retention; he could, and she'd seen him do it innumerable times, go through all manner of diverting, even disconcerting, situations, and when he spoke at all, pick up the exact skein of thought and conversation where he'd dropped it hours, even days, before. That was what he was doing now; blanking out everything that had occurred since they'd been sitting in the office at quitting time.

Undoubtedly, this was what made Sam Adams such a successful detective. It also, exasperatingly at times, made Helen Moran conscious that when he was engrossed with a riddle, she possessed only half a man. But she was too fond of Sam to be tart, and also she was too understanding about his work, being somewhat involved herself, not to appreciate his disciplined reactions.

But she still had no inkling about the reason Franz Ludwig had been killed, so her answer was predictable.

'I haven't the foggiest. Would he have been involved in something, Sam? Dope, maybe, counterfeiting, the numbers racket, moving stolen cars?'

Their meal came, it was delicious, Sam had a pint of stout along with it and Helen had tea, which she didn't especially like but the coffee at this English restaurant was unbelievable.

'Curly-head, Ludwig was a wraith. He

couldn't even remember his name. It would be like using a dog to deal cards in a poker game, using Ludwig for any of the things you've mentioned.'

'Well, Sam, I just don't know.' She smiled at him. She didn't have to know and they both were well aware of that. 'Do you know?'

He shook his head, ate a moment then grinned at her. 'But I'll find out. I'll tell you *how* I'll find out. Whoever was using Ludwig knew it was temporary; knew he couldn't rely on Ludwig, and knew Ludwig wouldn't live long. In the end he made sure of the latter, but I have a very strong hunch that before this someone used the gun, he also did something else: He tried his best to hasten Ludwig's exit.'

'Of course,' said Helen. 'Fed Mister Ludwig's habit.'

'Right. So tomorrow I'll go back down there and try to find out where Ludwig got the money he bought his wine with — besides what he received from his family. Somewhere, there'll be a man paying him off and watching him stagger around on the verge of self-destruction.'

'Did you read the Coroner's report?' asked Helen, and when Sam shook his head, saying something between mouthfuls about leaving it in the pocket of his other coat, she was very understanding; usually, people who concentrated on one thing as hard as Sam Adams concentrated on his assignments, were absent-minded. Not that it mattered. He had her.

'It said Mister Ludwig had been absorbing increasing amounts of liquor just lately. Do you see, Sam? That means you are right about someone trying to pump him so full he'd just collapse.'

'But he didn't collapse.'

'No although the report also says his system was so riddled and wrecked he couldn't have hung on more than perhaps another month or two.'

'Curly-head, does that tell you anything?'

'What, Sam?'

'Mister Somebody couldn't wait. Whatever Ludwig was involved with had to be completed quickly.'

'That could be just about anything felonious, couldn't it?'

Adams smiled and nodded. 'Sure. Even honest people like to complete business transactions and get on to the next one. But this also helps.'

Helen wasn't so sure of that but she didn't say so. She simply returned to her meal, and her tea, leaving Sam perhaps soaring around in his own world of deductive reasoning.

'What we have, then, Curly-head, is a wino killed because someone no longer needed him, but also because someone's timing about the wino dying unaided went sour, and because Mister Someone couldn't run the risk of having this completely unpredictable wino perhaps picked up by the police and wrung-out in some hospital, where he just might have remembered something he'd seen or done as he got back part of his rationale under treatment. And perhaps the key is something that had to be concluded swiftly.'

Helen, not required to do more than occasionally nod her head, managed during this oration to put away a good deal of her meal, finish her tea, and begin to feel wonderfully warm and replete.

'Tomorrow, then, you'll start looking for someone who gave Mister Ludwig money,' she said, 'and with whom he must have been seen by someone other than his skid-row friends. Right?'

'Right. And just one other thing. While I'm doing that, tomorrow, you'll be downstairs going over the reports filed by prowl-car crews and individual patrolmen for anything that happened in the area where Sauerkraut was hit.'

'Sam, why did they call Mister Ludwig Sauerkraut?'

'He was born in Germany and had a German accent. Not very pronounced but noticeable. His parents, his brother and sister also have accents. His parents worst of all. His brother and sister verified that he also had one. It's fairly common to call people with German accents something like that: Square-head, Kraut, or Sauerkraut. Well, what would you like for dessert?'

4

Prowling Skid-Row

Sam knew bartenders. Regardless of whether they were uptown or downtown, whether they excelled with *liqueur flambeau* or with dago red, and of course bartenders knew, if not Sam Adams specifically, cops. It was a matter of mutual recognition but nothing else.

The skid-row dive that had been pointed out the day before to Sam as Franz Ludwig's particular blind-pig had a powerful fragrance of disinfectant inside. It also had dark walls and a dark floor. It was not a very large place, its clientele never had much to spend, but profit-wise it was probable this saloon did more business than the cleaner joints uptown.

The barman was also the proprietor. His name was Pierre O'Gorman, which made for a nice, if incongruous, combination.

He told Sam he'd inherited the saloon from an uncle. He also told Sam that if he'd had any sense at all he'd have refused it. But he hadn't, and now he was sixty years old and winos no longer made him sick to his stomach.

'That's the way it goes. One day you can't keep nothing on your stomach, looking at 'em. The next day you eat like a horse an' sleep like a baby; you discover nothing changes, whether this bunch of saturated meat lives or dies. See?'

'Yeah. Pierre, try harder. They called him Sauerkraut. He was a skinny guy with a shock of wild dark hair.'

'Look, like I told you, Mister Adams, I serve two-thirds of 'em without looking up. They call an order, I put the glass in front of 'em, but I'm lookin' for the money. See?'

'A German accent, Pierre.'

'Don't mean a thing. I get 'em with every kind of — '

'Always had a little money. This past couple of weeks or so he had quite a bit.'

Pierre's vacant eyes steadied a little,

lingering on Sam's face. 'Okay,' he said. 'That's unusual. Let me think. 'Scuse me, there's a guy down the line needs a drink.'

Sam almost needed one himself. He'd pumped the patrolmen, had ambled around pumping other derelicts, had even sat in that abandoned old warehouse for an hour because he thought some of Sauerkraut's old cronies might come back. They never did.

He'd been in this saloon before too; no one at that time, including Pierre O'Gorman, had remembered Sauerkraut, but Sam had been certain this attitude had been prompted by caution; neither barmen nor derelicts, as a rule, had any use for a policeman. A detective in everyday clothing was even more suspect.

Pierre returned wiping his hands on a damp rag. 'Nope,' he said, before Sam could speak. 'If some guy was in here spending more money than usual the last week or so, I sure didn't notice it.' But Pierre wasn't altogether without encouragement. 'Look, bull, I got a suggestion. Forget it. If the dead guy was one of these,' O'Gorman waved a hand towards the motionless, hunched-forward filthy scarecrows perched on his bar-stools, 'he's better off dead than alive.'

Sam raised heavy brows. He'd heard that before. It didn't sound very convincing the other time either. Pierre, seeing the scepticism, tossed aside the sour bar rag and smiled weakly.

'Well, what's the best that can happen to 'em? They go to the drunk-tank with tremens, then to the hospital for drug treatment that's worse'n the tremens, they tell me, then right back here again, until some morning they wake up dead in an alley.'

Sam said, 'Thanks, Pierre. You've been a big help,' and walked back to his car. He hadn't been trying to sound sarcastic at all, Pierre *had* been a big help. Sam drove to the nearest precinct station, spent two hours copying names and dates, and disposition of cases, in a little notebook he carried, then he drove to the hospital where all chronic alcoholics were taken after

41

being sentenced to the cure by the courts.

Pierre had indeed encouraged Sam.

The orderly in the drunk-ward was an immense coloured man who seemed singularly devoid of the psychotic hang-ups of most coloureds. He greeted Sam with an easy grin, shook hands with a friendly grip, then listened gravely to everything Sam had to say. On his side, Sam told the coloured orderly more than he'd told Pierre; he explained *why* he wanted to find wrungout ones from Pierre's neighbourhood. The big orderly offered Sam a seat, sat at his tiny desk and systematically began pulling file cards.

It took fifteen minutes but when the scribbled list was complete the orderly handed it over with a grin. 'I'll go with you. It isn't that you're a cop; they won't know that. It's just that they know me.' He rose. 'Funny thing; they recognize me at once, even the black ones. I'm some kind of special image to 'em. But I wonder, was I out on the street and they passed me by what they'd think? Don't tell me. Well, let's go, we got seven from that area and directly it'll be time for me to start my rounds with the injections. If they don't get shot on schedule they start goin' up the walls. Nice, eh?'

It wasn't nice, of course, but on the other hand it was quiet, which drunk-tanks never were, and it was clean and airy.

Except that each patient had an identically wasted, shrunken appearance, each pair of eyes was empty and opaque, the ward could have been the domain of the legitimately ailing.

Oddly too, as the orderly had said, when he moved among them Sam saw the faint flickers of recognition and sluggish pleasure. He shook his head when the orderly grinned back.

Getting the derelicts to talk was not difficult, but getting them to talk about *specifics* required skill. They might start out listening carefully, even replying rationally, but within moments they were off on the most irrelevant and often irrational tangents. The big orderly never lost patience, never swore, never shook anyone with any exasperation. Sam was impressed, and because the big orderly was very skilled with these people, Sam left the initial questioning up to him.

But they drew blanks on the first three, and the fourth one was drowsily indifferent; he'd been heavily sedated an hour earlier when the imminence of delirium tremens had threatened to send him into paroxysms.

The fifth man surprised Sam with a clear and rational statement: 'Sauerkraut, sure I knew him. What of it?'

'He's dead,' said Sam, with the big orderly smiling encouragement at the bed-patient.

'All right,' said the alcoholic briskly. 'It's your ball-game, mister. So Sauerkraut is dead. We all go some time don't we?'

'You knew him well?'

'Well enough. What of that? You think I owed him money or something, mister?'

'No. Nothing like that. Who'd been giving him money lately?'

The alcoholic's swimming and faded gaze drifted to the big orderly. 'Jonas, how come you let this guy come in here and roust me; how about that, Jonas, for Crizzake?'

The orderly leaned, patted the wasted shoulder and said, 'Charley, this guy's a friend.'

'He looks like a cop to me, Jonas. How come you let a cop . . . Jonas, I always thought you was m'friend, and here you let a cop come in here and — '

'Charley, somebody killed this guy called Sauerkraut,' explained Jonas softly, bending low as though sharing a vital confidence. 'Now that isn't right, is it? Okay, so help Mister Adams, Charley. Man, it's you and me and this guy here against 'em all. So help a little, Charley; you dig?'

Charley swallowed painfully and two big tears coursed down into the creases of his cheeks. He looked back at Sam, 'Sure,' he croaked, and sniffled. 'Sure as hell, mister. We got to do this together, us three. I understand. What you want me to do?'

'Who was giving Sauerkraut money, Charley? Who did you see him with who didn't belong?'

45

'A couple of times there was this guy came to the warehouse. He'd bring some bottles, pass 'em round, then him and Sauerkraut'd go off in a corner for a minute or two.'

'What did he look like, Charley?'

A sudden spasm of irrational irritability seized Charley. He flung out skinny arms and swore shrilly. Jonas nodded and smiled, making no move to interfere. Sam sat back for the tantrum to pass. It did, then he repeated the question and Charley said, 'Young guy, nice dresser, drove a big black car he'd park outside. We could see it where boards was off the wall. Sort of lisped when he talked, had a kind of accent or something.' Charley paused for breath. He had more to relate but he also had the chronic breathlessness of the terminal alcoholic. 'I don't know what they talked about. Sauerkraut never said and we never asked. The guy brought us plenty to drink.'

That was the sum and substance of all Charley could say, and although Sam tried for another ten or fifteen minutes to get more from him, Charley simply

46

went back over the same ground again and again, until the big orderly caught Sam's eye and shook his head.

And it was time for Charley's next dose of sedation too.

Sam lingered up by the orderly-desk until Jonas finished his injections and returned. It was, he told the coloured man, better than nothing.

Jonas agreed. 'The guy you're lookin' for was young, flashy-dresser, had an accent an' drove a big car.' He laughed. 'Mister Adams, how many hundred-thousand guys around Manhattan would that fit?'

Sam smiled back. 'One hell of a lot, Jonas, except for one thing: How many with those qualifications will have police records, and of the ones with records, how many will be engaged in some kind of business that would take them down among the winos?'

Jonas thought that over. 'You know your business,' he averred. 'What do you do now?'

'Find all the suspects I can, get mug-shots of them and bring them back for

47

Charley to look at.'

Jonas's thoughtful expression turned a little wry. 'Mister Adams, don't wait too long.'

Sam kept thinking of those four words as he left the hospital, went to his car and started the drive back to his office. Charley would die soon. Franz Ludwig *would* have died soon too. Somewhere, there existed a very delicate mark of delineation. A bullet had killed Franz Ludwig, otherwise Sam Adams never would have heard of him. Society, or whatever it was that made men like Charley swim through amber alcohol to death, was also guilty of murder. What was the difference; why did a cop go forth to track down and incarcerate one killer and not the other one?

Sam entered the police building not too concerned with this interesting variation on right and wrong, saw Lieutenant Richard Stokes — Old Ironsides — nodded, and paced past to the stairway. Depending upon his mood, he walked to the second floor or he rode. Today he'd been walking a good deal, so he continued to do so.

When he entered the office Helen was absent. He peered over her typewriter at the mail-baskets, found nothing, saw her open dictation tablet with its shorthand gibberish, line after line, and went on through to his own office.

There, he sat down, brought forth the little book he'd made notes in, lit a cigarette and fell to studying what he'd turned up this day.

Of course the trouble with doing what he'd told the hospital orderly was his next step, was that although he would do it, and although it had sounded very professional exactly as the orderly had implied, nonetheless when it came down to gleaning worthwhile suspects Sam had no doubt but that he'd have a great armload to show Charley the alcoholic.

Charley could, undoubtedly, at one time have picked out the right face, but could he do that now, or would he irrationally, perhaps wearily and to get rid of Sam Adams, pick out the wrong one?

It wasn't a pleasant prospect. Failure never was. There was another small item:

Supposing Charley could *not* identify the suspect, or supposing he died before a positive identification could be made?

Helen came into the outer office, saw Sam hunched glum and motionless, threw him a little wave, a big smile, and, snatching up her dictation tablet, strode on in to face him across the desk. She looked as fresh and tomboyish at five in the afternoon as she must have looked at ten in the morning. It was quite an accomplishment, that.

'You told me to look into the reports filed for skid-row,' she said cheerily. 'Well, I've got them, Sam.'

He said, 'It's quitting time.'

She had an answer for that too. 'I know. But just so's no time will be lost, I'll take the tablet home with me, and you come over in an hour or so, and we'll have supper and go over what I have.'

5

A Dead Man Plus One

The average woman did not have to be much of a cook to be a better one than the average man was. Sam, whose apartment had a small kitchen including a stove, refrigerator, sink and cupboards, rarely used the kitchen at all, even though he kept the refrigerator partially full of his favourite variety of beer.

On the other hand, Helen, whose kitchen privileges were even smaller, was adept at making nourishing meals of the variety men ordinarily preferred. Nothing fancy; plenty of meat and potatoes and coffee. Ordinarily too, she had the ingredients on hand. If not, it only took a minute to pick them up on the way home, which is what she did this particular evening. But even so, by the time Sam Adams appeared she had a most wonderful aroma coming from her kitchen alcove.

She also had a drink for Sam, for which he was properly grateful, and when they ultimately sat in Helen's little dining nook, Sam was appreciatively hungry, which after all was the whole idea of getting him over there in the first place.

But he was also interested in whatever she'd dug up on skid-row arrests, so, as they started to eat, Sam brought the conversation to this point, where she dutifully took it up.

'Well, there was a fatal knifing. Any number of drunk arrests, two holdups, a warehouse burglary and one murder — Ludwig's.'

She raised a hand to bend a finger each time she made a point. 'The drunk arrests were routine. Likewise a couple of holdups. Incidentally, both felons were apprehended. That leaves — '

'A knifing,' said Sam, improperly speaking with his mouth full.

She sat, perhaps waiting for Sam to mention the other crime she hadn't dismissed, that burglary of a warehouse, but Sam returned to eating and said no more. She decided, for the sake of compatibility, to go along with the knifing, for the time being at least.

'He could have witnessed it,' she said, prompting Sam. It worked. He washed the food down with coffee and shook his head.

'It's not impossible, Curly-head, but suppose you fill me in with the details before I'm supposed to make some kind of judgement.'

'Yes, Sam. One of them was a Puerto Rican, the other was negro. The Puerto Rican survived, the negro did not. According to the Puerto Rican he was attacked by his adversary, a man named Hilton, over a bad debt, and the Puerto Rican only drew his blade when the negro already had a big knife in his hand.'

'Wait a minute,' Sam broke in, looking pained. 'Helen, there's nothing here that a witness would have to die to keep secret. Two men fighting with knives over an old debt, and one of them comes off second-best.'

She smiled. 'Ordinarily I'd be able to

hand you a rap-sheet at this point, with a great flourish, and prove you wrong. Not this time. The Puerto Rican has no record at all, although when I telephoned the immigration people they said he was not actually a Puerto Rican at all; that he came to the States from Puerto Rica, but originally he came from Matanzas Province in Cuba.'

Sam smiled, 'A spy. A Cuban infiltrator. An anarchist.'

Helen said, 'If he is, they must be getting a little desperate. He blew his cover when he knifed the negro.'

Sam dismissed the Puerto Rican. 'What of the dead negro?'

'He had a record all right. He was a trouble-maker, extortionist, mugger, imprisoned three times for aggravated assault.'

Sam took a swallow of coffee, put the cup down and shook his head. 'Even if Sauerkraut had witnessed all this violence, Curly-head, it strikes me as though the one person whose background indicates he might resent having a witness, was the loser.'

'Yes Sam.'

'What have you on the warehouse burglary?'

She brightened at once. 'It's *my* choice. Three men broke in two weeks ago. There is some feeling, at least it mentions it in the investigative report, that these burglars had broken into this same warehouse before, a month or more before this last burglary.'

'What did they get?'

'Bolts of Oriental brocade and very special silk. It was part of a shipment from a Hong Kong exporting firm to a Brooklyn retailer who deals in surplus stock, bankrupt inventories — anything that can be purchased at a price that guarantees a large profit. Nothing illegal; I looked up the company. It's called Asche and Cohn Associates. Has a good record with us and with the city as well.'

'Insured, Curly-head?'

'Yes. Under a blanket policy that protects anything coming inside the warehouse. Actually, Mister Asche told the investigating officers to forget it, there was no point in making an issue, the insurance people would pay off and that would be that.'

'Okay, but what did he tell them last time his place was burglarized?'

Helen blushed. 'I don't know, Sam. I didn't look into anything except this latest burglary.'

He was indulgent, and smiled over at her. 'It's my job anyway — except that I don't see any connection. Maybe the Asche and Cohn warehouse is down along the docks, Curly-head, but where does my lush come in?'

'As before, Sam, maybe he witnessed something?'

'Look. Something you've got to remember, Helen. My lush could have witnessed the original resurrection, and ten minutes later he couldn't have remembered a single thing about it.'

'Would those burglars know that, Sam? I mean, if they saw Mister Ludwig watching — '

'They'd have put a slug through his head right then and there, Curly-head. Look, what I've got to have before it even looks interesting, is something that ties Franz Ludwig to the burglars.'

Helen said, 'All right, Sam. That rag listed in Mister Ludwig's possessions as a very soiled handkerchief, was Oriental brocade.'

Sam sat motionless, gazing at Helen. He remembered the handkerchief, of course. That, some matches and a few pieces of silver money was all the corpse'd had on it.

'You're sure it was Oriental brocade,' he said, sounding a little annoyed.

'Yes, Sam. I went down and looked at it myself. It's in a big manila envelope down in the I.D. section.'

Sam finished his coffee, got free of the restrictive confines of the little eating nook and returned to the parlour where he sat, waited for Helen to join him, then said, 'Something is wrong, Curly-head. Granting that Ludwig witnessed the burglary, he wouldn't have told the police; he couldn't have remembered to tell us, or the event itself. So why kill him? Wait a minute — don't tell me they didn't know he was that far gone. You didn't have to be a psychologist to see that. They knew. Then why kill him?'

'It's got to be the risk, Sam.'

'Okay, I'll accept that for now, only I still don't believe it. As I said before, Curly-head, if it was the risk they wouldn't have let him live weeks after the burglary, would they?'

'Sam, I just don't know. I'm completely baffled. I made the notes this morning and kept going over and over them. It seems too inconsistent in some ways, but it also seems very rational another way.'

Sam was not that upset. He smiled at her. 'You did enough, Curly-head. In fact, you've actually turned up more on the case than I have.'

She was pleased, but sceptical. 'I have, Sam?'

'I couldn't put Sauerkraut anywhere, couldn't tie him to anyone. You found out the handkerchief was Oriental brocade. You tied him to your burglars and you also tied him to a specific event that very plausibly resulted in his death. Although I'll be damned if it makes very much sense right this minute.'

Still, and he admitted it before departing that night not too long after he'd eaten, if that rumpled, filthy bit of cloth found in the trouser-pocket of the corpse was indeed Oriental brocade, it would be extremely difficult for anyone to say it was coincidence, Franz Ludwig having a handkerchief of such stuff, and sound believable at all.

It did not at this time occur to Sam Adams that the theft of brocade and silk was anything more than a perfectly understandable theft of valuable cloth. It *did* occur to him the following morning when he was having that filthy scrap of cloth analysed, that he'd have to compare it with something to be positive it came from one of the missing bolts, and palpably, that wasn't going to be very simple. Even if the stolen cloth had been sold, it would still entail a lot of foot-work, and telephone-work also, to locate it again. Chances were, as Sam told Helen, that the cloth wouldn't surface within five hundred miles of New York.

She was slightly encouraging. 'Sam, not very many stores carry anything like that kind of cloth. The cost alone makes it prohibitive.'

Sam didn't dispute this statement, but neither did he choose to build his case on the missing brocade and silk. He got the address of the Hong Kong supplier from the insurance company — did not contact anyone connected with the Asche and Cohn Company — and sent an enquiry to British authorities in Hong Kong concerning both the exporter of that expensive cloth, and the cloth itself.

Then he went to work rounding up mug-shots of eligible suspects. He had little enough to use as a basis, but on the other hand, he had to start somewhere, so, with a very impressive envelope of head-on and profile photographs of men — not all young, although it was hinted the burglars had been youngish — he had a late luncheon, neglected to check in with Helen, which he usually did before leaving the building, and drove back to the hospital to have Charley make an identification — if he could.

He couldn't.

There were two uniformed officers

with Jonas at the entrance to the ward, and farther along two plain-clothes men were standing beside Charley's bed. Sam identified himself to the uniformed men, who did not know him, and although he recognized both the detectives down the room, he chose to face Jonas.

'What happened?'

'Someone shot him, Mister Adams.'

Sam stared at Jonas's black face. 'Shot — Charley?'

'Yes. In the head.'

Sam let all his breath out, stepped to the white chair behind Jonas and sank down. When the plain clothes men ambled on up, looking mildly surprised to find Sam sitting there, one of them said, 'He knew his business, but damned if it makes very much sense.'

Sam could dimly discern the slack, wasted frame under the bedding midway down the ward. 'It makes sense,' he growled, and looked up at the big coloured orderly. 'Jonas . . . ?'

The dark face came around. 'It happened during shift-change.'

Sam looked from the orderly to the

plain clothes men. No one volunteered anything so he asked the question he knew, from their faces, there was no answer to.

'Anyone see it happen; see anyone walk into the ward or walk out afterwards?'

They shook their heads and Sam leaned back in the chair gazing down where a department photographer was making his routine camera-work look very routine, indeed.

The plain clothes men left, heading for the hospital's office and records section. Jonas said, 'Mister Adams, it never occurred to me anything like this could happen.'

Sam nodded and rose, hugging his fat manila envelope, for which there now seemed no need at all despite the time he'd put in assembling its contents. He lit a cigarette ignoring the sign nearby prohibiting smoking.

Jonas had a question of his own. 'I came up with a little puzzler, Mister Adams. Charley was in here almost a week and no one even came near.'

Sam looked at the big coloured man.

'But I show up just once, and they zapped him. Right?'

'Yeah. Does it look like that to you too?'

'It does.'

'Why?'

'I don't know, Jonas, except that someone heard about me nosing around where Franz Ludwig was killed yesterday, tailed me to the hospital, and . . . ' Sam smiled thinly. 'You're the only one who knows I talked to Charley. Did that occur to you too?'

'Yes, it crossed my mind. But you and I both know something else, Mister Adams: You didn't get any identification out of Charley, did you?'

Sam looked round for a place to put out his cigarette. Jonas supplied a glass ashtray from a desk-drawer. 'Nope,' exclaimed Sam, 'Charley wasn't much help. But maybe someone figured I'd come back with pictures for Charley to look at. Maybe they guessed Charley could identify someone.'

Jonas shrugged, gazing down where the photographer was still working. 'Well, they could have been wrong, y'know, because I wouldn't have bet a dime on your chances of getting Charley to identify anyone you showed him.'

'They didn't like the risk, Jonas. They didn't like it with Franz Ludwig either.'

'Man,' said Jonas softly, 'they sure play for keeps, don't they? Charley never would have left this ward under his own power. But they hit him anyway. Bad people to be messed up with, eh?'

Sam agreed that they were, indeed, very bad people to be involved with. And he could have added something that might have wiped away Jonas's expression of brooding disapproval, but he didn't add it for a simple reason: He had something else in mind for Jonas.

It wouldn't have done a bit of good to explain to Jonas that *he* was in trouble; he'd been with Sam Adams at the interrogation of Charley the day before. Charley may, or may not, have told the police something, and now Charley was dead. But Jonas was still very much alive.

Sam thanked Jonas for what little help

he'd been, nodded to the uniformed policemen who were still by the doorway into, and out of, the ward, took his manila envelope and ambled away.

He telephoned Helen from the hospital's personnel room where he'd just copied down an address, saying he wouldn't be back at all for the rest of the day, then went out and climbed into his car with the fat manila envelope on the seat beside him.

6

A Surprised Orderly

Jonas came down the sidewalk in a dark turtleneck sweater and a checked sports coat, looking like almost anything but an orderly in the drunk-ward of a hospital.

Sam leaned and called softly. 'Jonas . . . ? Over here. Sam Adams.'

Jonas came, leaned far down, looked at Sam in total surprise and flashed white teeth as he said, 'Man, cop or no cop, this isn't the healthiest part of town for a white guy at night. This is dark-town.'

Sam heaved the door open. 'Get in,' he said, not heeding anything Jonas had said. 'Close the door.' As Jonas obeyed Sam started the sedan, eased from the kerbing and said, 'Where's a decent restaurant?'

Jonas shook his head, then grinned a little. 'Straight ahead a few blocks, I'll show you.' He didn't ask why Sam had waylaid him. He said nothing more about the unpleasant things that occasionally happened to whites, cops or otherwise, in the black-man part of town. In fact, until they strolled into the clean little cafe he'd directed them to, he didn't say anything at all.

They got a back table. They also got some stony stares but Jonas wasn't very concerned. 'Soreheads,' he explained. 'See those beards and beads? Well, every white guy's got to be a honkie to those types.'

A pretty sepia waitress came. Jonas grinned. 'One thing, Mister Adams, no one believes in using poison yet.' He winked at the girl. 'Couple of orders of meatloaf, coffee, and whatever pie is freshest.'

Sam put the manila envelope on the table, offered Jonas a smoke, held a match for them both, then said, 'Did you have any other ideas today, Jonas?'

'Like what?'

'Like Charley is dead and he talked to me. You're alive, and you also talked to me.'

Jonas stopped smiling, blew smoke, then softly said, 'I understand the cloak-and-dagger pick-up as I walked home, now. I appreciate your thoughtfulness. And no — I didn't come up with anything like you just suggested. Why should they want to zap me? Even if Charley'd told you something, just being an eavesdropper wouldn't implicate me — would it?'

'I don't know, Jonas. But I'll tell you something; if I were in your shoes I wouldn't go for any late-night walks for a while.'

'Nice, man,' said Jonas, stubbing out his cigarette and looking solemn. 'What in the hell is it all about? What'd this Ludwig-character do?'

Sam had no answer so he gave none. He opened the manila envelope and spilled out the pictures. 'Look them over, carefully. I think you've probably seen one of these men. I think it's very probably he has also seen you.'

'Yeah. *And* you think he got to Charley, right?'

'Possibly. One other question, Jonas:

68

How could it be timed so well — right at shift-change?'

'Easy. Anyone who's ever visited the ward at seven in the morning or seven at night would see the change. To verify it, he'd only have to show up a couple more times.'

Sam smiled. 'That's exactly my idea, Jonas.' He pointed at the photographs Jonas was picking up and arranging in his hands. 'One of these men probably did that, and very recently. Maybe yesterday morning or last night. You look through 'em and pick out the man I'm looking for.'

Jonas smiled at Sam. 'You're pretty tricky at that.' He leaned back as the sepia waitress returned with their meal, and after she'd gone again Jonas began examining the pictures slowly and meticulously.

Sam ate, made no attempt to interrupt, and privately cursed his lousy luck. Of all the hospital wards he had to get involved with, it had to be one full of people whose minds had been turned to jelly. Otherwise, someone who'd seen that assassin enter, walk half the length of the ward, shoot Charley — with a silencer, obviously — would have been shouting his head off by now. Instead, they all lay exactly as they always lay, like vegetables. They breathed and spoke, ate a little, functioned like human beings, saw a murder committed and were just as blankly sedated as before.

Jonas looked up. 'Do I call you sergeant? Mister Adams sounds pretty . . . ' He shrugged massive shoulders 'You understand?'

'Yeah. Sam will do fine. Which one?'

'Sam — sorry; if I've ever seen one of these men before I surely don't remember it. Not around the hospital in the past few days. I'd remember that.'

'So — he knew the shift-change that well, Jonas. He waited, timing your predecessor, then slipped in while your predecessor was out and before you came on duty. Very good, wouldn't you say?'

'Yes, very good Sam, all of a sudden I'm beginning to wonder if this guy with the silencer can also walk through the locked door of my flat'

70

'You can have protective custody if you like. Or I can assign a couple of plain clothes men.' Sam looked steadily at the big orderly. 'Would you like some advice? Don't rely on bodyguards. No one ever sees in all directions at the same time. If these people really want to get you, they will do it no matter how many bodyguards you have.'

Jonas lit another cigarette, pushed his half-eaten meal aside and said, 'Yeah. I saw how they did it with Bobby Kennedy. With the President. Okay, but Sam, protective custody messes me up even more.'

'Why? Do you have a family?'

'Nothin' like that. I'm single and footloose. But how do I work at the ward if I'm hiding out in some jail cell?'

Sam nodded. 'You could still go to work. You'd just spend the nights at — '

'Sam, they could get me easy that way — in my ward while I'm on duty.'

That was true and Sam didn't deny it, although he suggested that bodyguards in the ward might be more efficient than they'd ever be on the sidewalk.

Jonas grimaced. 'That'd be something, wouldn't it? An orderly in a drunk-ward needing police protection.'

Sam ate, drank coffee, let Jonas arrive at his own decision in his own way, and when it looked as though he might be having trouble, Sam said, 'Take a ride with me; finish your dinner.'

'I am finished. Where are we going?'

'I want to show you some mug-books.'

'Hell man, if I couldn't pick him out of this select group what chance . . . ?'

'Listen to me, Jonas. I don't want you dead any more than you want to *be* dead.'

'Soul-brother,' murmured big Jonas, and grinned.

Sam didn't pay any attention to the amused sarcasm. 'I want you to keep looking at pictures.' Jonas started to speak and Sam headed him off. 'Listen. Just listen. Maybe you recognize someone, maybe you don't. I'm not too concerned about that. *But someone else will be, Jonas.* Do you understand? You are very likely already on someone's hit-list. Okay. I mean to exploit that to the hilt, to find my killer. You're all I have at present. Like it or not, Jonas, you're involved. As long as someone thinks you might be able to identify him, or say something perhaps that Charley confided in you after I left the ward yesterday, you're involved up to your ears.'

'Bait,' murmured Jonas, and let the waitress remove the plates in front of him. 'It's not your fault, is it? Nor mine. Nor Charley's fault. Nor this other one — the guy they called Sauerkraut. But you're right, Sam, I'm involved, and it's too damned risky, hoping — like I'm doing hard right this minute — you're all wrong about someone thinking they'd better zap me too. It's okay taking a chance at cards or dice — but man — this is my *life*, and that's pretty scary, isn't it?'

Sam arose, dropped some notes on the table and waited for Jonas to slide up out of the booth too. As they turned to leave the little place they got those same stony stares again, and neither of them paid the slightest attention.

The sky had turned dark while they'd

been in the little restaurant. They went to the police sedan and climbed in. Sam said that if Jonas wished, they could go first to his flat. Jonas shook his head about that, so Sam headed out into the night time traffic heading towards his office in the detective section of Police Headquarters.

Jonas asked, again, what it was all about, and of course, except for the little additional information he'd picked up since the day before, Sam really couldn't be very enlightening. Jonas persisted. He said, 'It's got to be something, Sam. People don't walk into hospitals and kill other people without . . . Hey; maybe one of the other orderlies, or one of the nurses, saw this guy who zapped Charley. I mean, man, my ward's up a flight of stairs. This guy had to come up in the lift or he came up the stairs.'

Sam had already considered that. He was wheeling into the parking area out back of his building when he said, 'Sure, *someone* saw him, Jonas. Maybe a lot of people saw him. But we can't take everyone on duty when Charley was killed, bring them in here and make them sit around looking at mug-books hour after hour. What I've got to do first, is identify this man. Tack a name and description on him.'

'How, if no one's seen him up close?'

'You're forgetting what Charley said, Jonas. The guy lisped or had an accent. Flashy-dresser.'

'Sam that ain't much, and my neck depends on you finding this bird real fast.'

'I'll find him,' said Sam, pointing the way. 'That's not my problem right now.' He grinned as he held the door for Jonas to precede him inside. 'My problem is to get *him* before he gets *you*.'

'That's hilarious,' said Jonas, and followed Sam Adams all the way to the Identification and Files Bureaux without saying another word.

The night-clerk, a young man with a pleasant, open face, showed them where the coffee urn was, made a table available, then faded out.

Sam got some books for Jonas to browse through, then started returning the photographs he'd borrowed to their proper slots. It was a tedious undertaking, but Sam was fed, not especially tired yet, and a little hopeful that Jonas might inadvertently turn up something.

Jonas did. He came upon the photograph of a neighbour of his, and laughed aloud over that. 'This bird's a lay-preacher at the neighbourhood church. Man, look at the record he's got!'

Sam couldn't have cared less. He went along to his office with a sneaking hunch Helen might have left a note or two. It was a good hunch. She'd left a typed page quoting a teletype from the Hong Kong authorities. The export firm involved in sending Asche and Cohn Associates the brocade and silk was listed as being an old and reliable firm with contacts in all the world's major cities. There was no record of any improprieties, but the Hong Kong police were careful to point out that since their port-city was the chief source of contact between Communist China and the West, it was never altogether safe to say an individual person or an individual business concern was absolutely above reproach.

As for the imported cloth, the British authorities reported that a cursory investigation revealed that the bolts had been in a local warehouse for several months, and at this time they were unable to report where they'd originally come from. They said they would continue looking into the matter, and if anything worthwhile cropped up, they would notify Sam Adams.

It was all a very concise, polite, brisk communication but it didn't tell Sam a damned thing. He stuffed it in his pocket, read another note Helen had left, advising him there was to be another meeting upstairs the following afternoon, then he left the office, lit a smoke out in the hall and began speculating about that cloth. If it were so rare and coveted, why had someone let it lie in a Hong Kong warehouse for several months?

He decided to go and visit Asche and Cohn Associates on the morrow, and strode along to make arrangements for Jonas to spend his first night in protective custody. It amused him, for some reason, thinking of Jonas's reaction to this.

It was close to nine o'clock, there was a pleasant aroma of coffee throughout the building, and although plenty of teletypes clattered, telephones jangled and men's raised voices echoed along the hallways, the building was not nearly as bustling as it was on a normal working day.

Sam began to feel tired. Some of it doubtless had to do with the rude shock he had received at the hospital earlier. More of it was simply the result of a long, trying day when he hadn't really accomplished anything.

He headed for the identification room after arranging for the cell, and told himself that the taxpayers — bless their little peaked heads — were damned well getting their money's worth, whether he managed to pull a rabbit out of the hat every day or not.

7

Saturated Trouble!

He started out the next morning as though it were just another routine day.

He drove to Asche and Cohn Associates office, beside their recently burgled warehouse, met Mister Cohn — Mister Asche was out of the city for a few days on a selling trip — and discovered a mild attitude of annoyance.

'I told your people,' said Mister Cohn, who was short, fat, balding, and ferret-faced, 'the cloth was insured. Look, we have these things happen every now and then. I'm not blaming the police, you understand. What I'm saying is that we pay a hell of a premium for insurance. It's the insurance people who say the police coverage of this dock area stinks — not me. Anyway, we been reimbursed for the silk and brocade. So what's the big rub?'

Sam could have said the big rub was murder. Instead, he played the part of an out-sized penitent and let Mister Cohn get it all off his chest. Finally, he wanted to know if Asche and Cohn Associates had already sold that cloth.

Cohn said, 'Yes. As a matter of fact we been trying like hell to get it delivered for two months. The shipping out of the Orient is lousy.'

'Who bought it — sight unseen, Mister Cohn?'

'Not sight unseen, Mister Adams. We got some swatches of the stuff and sold the bolts off them. The buyer was an outfit on the West Coast. In San Francisco. Hyman Company Imports.'

'You've done business with them before?'

'A few times, yes. But they aren't one of our steady outlets. And — we had to send back the deposit.' Cohn shrugged. 'So now we're trying to get more of the cloth — this time to be sent air-freight.'

'And it may be stolen again.'

'Too much of a coincidence, Mister Adams,' said Cohn, looking sardonic.

'Next time they'll hit us for sacks of coffee or maybe silverware. I only wish we could afford our own patrolmen.'

Sam left Mister Cohn, drove back to Pierre O'Gorman's gin-mill, and got an odd look from the proprietor as he eased his bulk down upon a rickety bar-stool. O'Gorman sidled up and said, 'Charley too?'

Sam nodded.

O'Gorman said, 'That's not so good. Sauerkraut, I figured just got in someone's way. Those things can happen around this neighbourhood. Only now it's beginning to look a little different. Well, isn't it?'

'Yeah,' sighed Sam. 'Have you remembered who the flashy-dresser is who talks with a lisp?'

'No.'

'Have you asked around?'

'Do I look crazy? *I* don't get paid for sticking my neck out, *you* do.'

'But there's been talk, Pierre. If you've heard that Charley got it too, so have others. What do they say?'

'Look at 'em,' replied O'Gorman,

81

making that same contemptuous gesture towards his silent, scarecrow patrons again. 'If they heard they don't remember *what* they heard. I'll tell you something; this doesn't make much sense to me. You don't have to shoot these people, they kill themselves a little each day.'

'Someone had to shoot them,' said Sam, sliding off the rickety stool. Then, feeling unaccountably malicious, he added: 'And if this lad feels compelled to shoot the jelly-heads, Pierre, you'd better hope he doesn't suddenly decide a guy like you, who is rational, is dangerous to him too.'

After leaving O'Gorman's tavern Sam went cruising the area until he located the squad-car. The patrolmen remembered him as the detective who'd been asking questions about Sauerkraut. They were curious about what he'd turned up. He only gave them what information he thought they'd have guessed anyway, mainly about Charley getting killed in the hospital-bed, then he said, 'Keep an eye on O'Gorman's wino-dive. I'm not saying I have anything to back that up.

I haven't. But it's possible that whoever killed the other two will try again.'

The grizzled, elder patrolman was sceptical. 'O'Gorman? If there was ever a nobody, he's it. He's as fuzzy in his own way, as his patrons are in their way.'

'Probably, but all the same . . .'

'Yeah, okay,' said the grizzled patrolman with a little shrug.

Sam left the area heading for his office. He hadn't seen Helen in what was a long time, and then there was Jonas. He had no illusions about the reception he'd get from that quarter.

Fortunately, he saw Jonas first. Otherwise he might have overlooked Jonas. And the reception he got wasn't really as yeasty as he'd expected, although Jonas was a little nettled because Sam still hadn't come up with a name, a worthwhile suspect.

It was later in the afternoon when he finally drove into the police parking area after a late lunch at a ptomaine parlour up town, and ambled on up to his office, that this very ordinary, routine day turned into something else.

Helen was waiting, pert as usual and tom-boyish, except that her expression was grave when she greeted him, and the paper she drew from a drawer to thrust at him in lieu of a smile was a mild bombshell.

'From the laboratory,' she explained. 'That brocade and silk was a lot more valuable than we thought. It was saturated with a heroin secretion.'

Sam dropped upon the chair beside Helen's desk and scowled. 'It was what?'

'Read the lab report. The cloth, all the bolts of it, had been saturated in a heroin secretion. The lab people say this is something they've never encountered before. Evidently someone in the Orient has devised a method of soaking cloth in a heroin solution, drying the cloth, putting it up in bolts just like any other cloth, and when someone gets it over here, they re-soak it using catalytic agents in the soak, and re-claim the heroin. It's diluted, of course, but then they have to dilute it anyway since a straight shot of heroin is fatal. And I would assume, as the lab people have, that being of reduced strength, it sells for a reduced price.'

Sam felt round in his coat for smokes, lit one, leaned forward and read the laboratory report slowly and thoroughly. It said about what Helen had just told him, but in a more formal and technical manner.

He re-read it.

Helen answered the telephone, promised to give Sam a message, rang off and said, 'You missed that meeting this afternoon. The chief would like you to come up right now — if you can.'

Sam leaned back with the laboratory report in his hand, gazing over at her as though he hadn't heard a word she'd said. 'I never heard of such a thing,' he said. 'They got all this off that piece of brocade Franz Ludwig was using as a handkerchief.'

'Yes. Sam; that was Lieutenant Stokes on the telephone just now. He and the chief are waiting for you upstairs.'

'Okay,' Sam said, but he didn't move. '*Now* it's beginning to make sense.'

'You'll have to alert the narcotics people in Washington. Would you like me to take care of that?'

'Yes. And now I've got to find where that damned cloth went, too.' He rose, stuffed the laboratory report in his pocket and went to the door. 'Listen, Curly-head, look up a copy of that report from the Hong Kong authorities. Send them the information about this saturation process for impregnating cloth with heroin. They ought to love hearing that story. Also, ask them for any names they can come up with of people — Americans — who have recently contacted anyone they can tie to those bolts of cloth.'

Sam left the office, went to the lift, rode to the fourth floor and encountered Lieutenant Richard Stokes looking as grim as death, in the hallway just outside the lift, when Sam stepped forth.

Stokes glowered. 'I was on my way down to get you. What happened that made you miss the meeting this afternoon?'

Sam fished forth the laboratory report, handed it over, and as Stokes read, they both walked back towards a closed metal door with Chief Of Detectives emblazoned across the upper part of it.

Stokes cursed softly as Sam held the door for him to pass inside, then he turned and said, 'It's ingenious, Sam.'

The Chief of Detectives, Captain John Hall, was a grey, dour, pipe-smoking man addicted to baggy tweed suits and military haircuts. He scowled at Sam Adams and might have said something unpleasant except that Lieutenant Stokes handed him the laboratory report, which Captain Hall bent his head to scrutinize as he vigorously puffed his pipe. Afterwards, he curtly waved Sam and Richard Stokes to chairs, went behind his desk and said, 'Well, and where is this silk, Sam?'

'I have no idea, sir.'

'But you're on it, aren't you?'

Sam toyed with the truth a little by nodding. 'I'm on it, Captain, but I just saw that report no more than fifteen minutes ago.'

'There is a connection between this man Ludwig and the contraband cloth?'

'I don't think there's much doubt about that, sir, but at this moment I can only speculate about the connection.'

'Ludwig was probably part of the crew that stole the cloth.'

Sam, who had served under John Hall six years, knew better than to contradict the man. He said, 'Ludwig was involved, I'm fairly certain.' He then told of the murder of the alcoholic called Charley, in the drunk-ward of the general hospital, which stopped both Hall and Stokes in their tracks. Stokes, recovering first, said, 'Sam, I'll give you more men.'

Captain Hall leaned to pass the laboratory report back and afterwards removed his pipe, put it aside and gave his head a hard wig. 'What else?' he growled. 'How close are you to them, Sam?'

That was another sticky question. It never did much good, saying one was close, because, if called upon to elucidate, the truth didn't close much of a gap. 'I have a man in protective custody,' replied Sam, then turned to Lieutenant Stokes. 'I can use a couple of men to cover this individual, and to also cover a tavern-keeper down on skid-row.'

Captain Hall rose. 'Get on it right

away, gentlemen. And keep me informed.'
He didn't mention the meeting Sam had
missed, which was the usual weekly skull-
session, at all.

Even when Sam and Lieutenant Stokes
were riding back down to the second
floor in the lift, this event was not
mentioned. But when they stepped forth
into the gloomy, lysol-scented corridor
Stokes — Old Iron-sides — fastened his
uncompromising stare upon Sam and
said, 'You are lucky you had this mess
to come up with. He was mad as a hornet
when everyone showed up but you. Next
time I doubt if you'll be able to come up
with a suitable encore, Sam. Now then,
about those men; will you need them this
afternoon?'

'As soon as they're available, Lieutenant.'

Stokes nodded. 'I'll have them sent
around right away. And Sam, keep me
informed.'

Back in his own office again, Sam blew
out a big breath of relief, but when Helen
looked up enquiringly he didn't say what
the big sigh was about. Instead, he asked
if she'd got off the message to the British

authorities in Hong Kong.

She had. And she was curious about the reaction that laboratory report had caused upstairs. Sam said it was, in a way, an unexpected and very welcome diversion. Then he glanced at his watch, saw how close it was to quitting time, and asked if she'd care to go round to their other favourite restaurant — the Hungarian goulash palace — after work.

She smiled the way he was accustomed to seeing her when he was around the office, said she'd sneak out a bit early so as to be ready when he came round to pick her up, and told him, apropos of nothing they'd been discussing, that he looked weary.

He reflected upon that for a moment, and might have had a comment to make about it, except that two strapping young plain clothes men strode into the office at this juncture, saying they'd been re-assigned to him for instructions.

He sent one officer to keep a protective eye on Pierre O'Gorman, and detailed the other one to look after the coloured orderly in the drunk-tank of the general hospital. As they departed, with all the instructions and general information they'd need, he winked at Helen, said he too was going to sneak away early this afternoon, and walked out — forgetting his hat again.

8

Some Vague Suspicions

Hungarian cooking was, or so Sam commented to Helen over their meal, rather similar to Mexican cooking. At least the Hungarians were addicted to spicy condiments and a striving towards epicurean innovation, too.

But the food was good. Helen was pleased with it and Sam, with something else on his mind, absently agreed when the waiter asked if their meal was entirely satisfactory.

As soon as the waiter had departed Sam said, 'I'm curious about the British reaction.'

To anyone but Helen that might have implied almost any kind of international repercussion. Helen smiled. 'Surprise, I imagine, Sam. Unless of course they already know about this saturation process.'

Sam doubted that they did. 'The

information would have been passed along. My guess is that the process is something new.'

Helen, always agreeable, accepted Sam's surmise. 'The lab report mentioned a slow process at both ends, with some risk of loss involved. But Sam, it seemed to me as I read that paper, there is more than enough money involved for people to innovate, if they could just keep from being caught and from having their contraband seized.'

'That's always been the problem,' exclaimed Sam. 'Selling the junk once it's in the country is dangerous of course, but *getting it in* is the real stickler. And this new process may be the answer. We won't know, I don't suppose, until we get our hands on someone connected with the racket, just how many bolts of cloth have been brought through Customs.'

'Did Franz Ludwig have a hand in it, Sam?'

They exchanged a look. Helen's face, as she asked that question, reflected more doubt than anything else, and Sam seemed a trifle baffled.

'That brocade handkerchief cost him his life, Helen, but that's about all I am sure of right now. Still, according to everyone who should know, Ludwig *couldn't* have been a very active participant.'

'What do you think, then?'

'If I knew where he got that handkerchief, I'd have an idea of the degree of Franz's involvement.'

For a while they ate and said nothing. Apart from some private thoughts, a man with a violin came by their table playing some lilting song, from the sound of it perhaps of gypsy origin, so they couldn't have talked if they'd wanted to, and afterwards, when he leaned to say that he wondered if the Asche and Cohn company was actually involved, some boisterous people at an adjoining table burst into the lyrics of the song their troubador was playing, and that very effectively drowned out all other sound.

Later, outside in the pleasant but oniony-scented night, Sam tried again. 'Asche and Cohn don't have to be involved. I think, if they *were*, there wouldn't have been a robbery; they wouldn't draw attention to themselves or the brocade and silk. But — *someone* knew, obviously, when the cloth would arrive and which warehouse it'd be stored in. Perhaps there's an Asche and Cohn employee who is part of the crew that reclaims the dope. It's just as possible, however, that no one over here knew, except the men who burgled the warehouse, made off with the cloth — and who also killed Ludwig and Charley.'

'That is what I don't understand,' said Helen, and Sam hustled her to the car, closed the door on her and as he slid in beside her, he punched the starter-button.

'There *is* a connection,' he said. 'I'm going to show you what it is.'

He drove down into the foul-smelling area of skid-row. Helen may have lost all interest as soon as she saw the staggering, filthy human wrecks down there, the little dark taverns, the littered streets and gaunt old unclean buildings, but if this were so the only indication of it was the way she sidled closer to Sam as he parked the car not far from O'Gorman's gin-mill and helped her out.

Two gaunt figures materialized out of a doorway, hands outstretched, faces leering, dirt-encrusted clothing threadbare almost to the point of disintegration. From a distance of six feet the smell was sour-sweet and nearly overpowering. Sam hastily handed them both some coins and turned away with Helen clinging to his arm. The wraiths turned abruptly, heading with jerky steps towards O'Gorman's place.

Sam took her down where the Asche and Cohn warehouse stood, explained that this was where the cloth had been stolen, then he walked her to another warehouse, not too distant, which was where Franz Ludwig had been found shot to death.

'My guess is that Ludwig either accidentally or on purpose got in the wrong warehouse.'

'Of course,' she said. 'He saw them break in and steal the saturated cloth.'

Sam smiled and shook his head. 'No. They'd have killed him on the spot if they'd found him in there the night they stole the cloth. I think what happened was that Ludwig, needing a handkerchief, tore off that piece of brocade from one of the saturated bolts, possibly several nights before they came to burglarize the Asche and Cohn warehouse and steal the stuff.'

'Then how would they know Ludwig had that scrap of brocade?'

'I've told you about Charley, the one they shot in the hospital. He wasn't as far gone in the head as the others. He was pretty bad, but not totally blank yet. They found a piece gone off their brocade, asked around, ran into Charley who named Sauerkraut as the person having that very elegant handkerchief, and went after him.' Sam paused a moment, then said, 'I'm only guessing, Curly-head, and there are some missing pieces, but it had to be about like this.'

'Sam, they didn't have to *kill* Mister Ludwig. You've said that yourself.'

'That is one of the missing pieces, Curly-head.'

He took her back up where they'd left the car and found a patrol car parked in front of their sedan, its little revolving dome-light flashing amber. The officers, two in number, were standing idly, waiting. They had already verified that Sam's sedan was a police vehicle but the sight of Sam *and* Helen made both patrolmen raise their brows.

'Anything wrong?' asked a large, burly officer whose nose showed signs of having been broken more than once, and whose steady eyes studied Sam with close but veiled interest.

Sam assured them that as far as he knew, nothing was wrong. He explained that he was involved in the murder of the wino called Sauerkraut, which seemed to prompt a little interest in the uniformed men. The second officer, leaner but just as tall and heavy-boned as his partner, said, 'Yeah, we were told there was a plain clothes man staked out on O'Gorman's place. Is there more to the Ludwig thing than just a killing over a wine bottle?'

'That burglary at the Asche and

Cohn warehouse,' said Sam. 'There is a connection.'

The officer with the flattened nose looked dubious. 'They don't very often burglarize, when they get as far along as Ludwig was. Don't have the strength, nor the ability to concentrate.'

Sam was patient. 'I know. Did you happen to know one of them called Charley; skinny little guy, maybe fifty or fifty-five years old, grey and — '

'Yeah, we knew Charley,' acknowledged the older officer, touching the tip of his flattened nose with that lingering look of scepticism. 'He'd only been down here a year or so. Tougher than the rest, too. Not so far gone.'

'Someone shot him in the drunk-tank at General Hospital.'

The two policemen hadn't heard this, evidently, because their sceptical looks vanished to be replaced by looks of incredulity. The rawboned younger man said, '*Shot* him; why would someone do that?'

'If I was sure of that,' responded Sam Adams, 'I'd be farther along with this mess than I am now.' He guided Helen to the door of the sedan, opened it for her, closed it after her and threw a final look at the patrolmen.

'Anything interesting been happening tonight?'

The man with the battered nose shook his head. 'Quiet, like always.'

'No drunk arrests?'

'No. We have a system. Everybody down here is drunk. If we hauled them in every night for being drunk in public, or drunk-loitering, or any of the other code regulations, we'd be operating a shuttle-bus from here to the cells. So we got a system; we don't bother them unless there is a big fight, or unless they start passing out in the middle of the streets, or unless they get too bold and start panhandling out of their district.' The officer smiled at Sam humorously. 'Live and let live, sort of.'

Sam drove away from there with a cynical expression. 'I guess that's how it has to work,' he told Helen. 'What makes them that way?'

'Psychosis,' she promptly replied. 'I

read a book about alcoholics one time.' She sidled closer to him on the seat as the car worked its way back up where there was more traffic, more lights, more presentable people. 'They are people who can't adjust or conform. There's something out of kilter in their makeup. They can be too gentle or too sensitive, or even too self-conscious and timid.'

'Any cure?' he asked, avoiding another car, that shot out of a dark side-street, with inches to spare.

She sighed and said, 'No *general* cure. No one-shot cure for all of them, and that's the difficulty; each one requires separate attention. We don't have the facilities nor the trained people.'

'Just as well,' he sighed. 'What would it cost in doctors and maintenance, per individual lush? Thousands of dollars a year, probably, and for what? You'd have a damaged brain and a short-circuited body jerking around in a dog-eat-dog world where even the perfectly co-ordinated don't always make it.'

'Sam, you ought to be ashamed. It isn't

101

right to just let them die, is it?'

He thought of something he'd heard. 'Why isn't it? Maybe they're better off dead.'

They arrived out front of her building, which was mostly dark, he switched off the ignition and sat staring straight ahead, with both big hands still gripping the wheel.

'Do you know what I think, Helen? I think the people who had Charley killed knew what they were doing.'

'Sam, you said yourself that he couldn't in all probability have identified anyone.'

'That's right. But I think Charley knew perfectly well how Sauerkraut got into the Asche and Cohn warehouse; I'll bet Charley knew how to get in there too. *That's* why they knocked him off. Because they figured sooner or later he would mention getting into that warehouse.'

Sam slapped the steering-wheel, twisted and looked down. Helen smiled up at him very invitingly. He swung away, opened his car door, climbed ponderously out, went round to her side and held the door for her to also alight. Then, taking her arm, he steered her to the lift inside the building, and there he said, 'I should have guessed that before, Helen.'

'Sam, you can't always guess ahead.'

'I should have this time, Curly-head.' He watched the lift-door automatically open. 'If I hadn't been bogged down with the details I might have been able to prevent what happened to Charley.'

'Does that mean you can prevent Mister O'Gorman and that hospital orderly from being injured?'

'It means, Curly-head, no one's going to injure those two.'

'I don't follow you, Sam.'

He turned, guided her into the lift, smiled benignly at her and reached over to push the button that would activate the lift. 'See you in the morning, Curly-head.'

'Thanks for the dinner, Sam.' The door clanked closed, and as the lift lurched, she added something else, but Sam was already hastening back towards the car.

'You're as strong as oak, Sam-love, and twice as thick!'

It was past ten o'clock when Sam turned to head back in the direction of skid-row. It didn't make much sense, returning to that area so late at night, for even the sleepless denizens would by now be hopelessly juiced-up.

But Sam didn't have in mind asking questions. He drove directly to the Asche and Cohn warehouse, parked across the way and with the torch from his glove-compartment, walked over to make a slow and careful circuit of the weathered old building.

Getting inside, he discovered, didn't involve special burglar tools; it didn't even involve great physical strength. Where rotting siding had crumbled other boards had been nailed over, and where careless truckers had backed into the walls, there were gaping cracks. Even a man as large and thick as Sam was, could, with very little straining, pry aside enough old planking to get into the warehouse.

He did it without so much as snagging his coat on old rusty nails.

9

A Bolt of Brocade

That easy access answered one question — why Sauerkraut and perhaps other winos started using the Asche and Cohn warehouse — and it also suggested at least a theoretical answer to another question — why the men who stole that impregnated cloth used this particular warehouse.

There might also have been another reason; aside from being easily accessible, it also was in a part of the city people simply did not visit after dark.

Sam didn't use his hand-torch for a long while. The warehouse was huge, there were plenty of cracks for moonlight to filter through, and over near the boxed-off section where the offices were, a night-light shielded in thick wire cast a gloomy glow part way across the width of the structure.

There was room in the building for ten times the freight that was stacked in the centre of the place. There had once been aisles, denoted by faded yellow paint, evidently for warehousemen to use in storing crates, but now, with less than a third of the ground-area being used, there was no need to observe the floor-rules; at least no one did observe them because the mounded merchandise in the warehouse at this time was all stacked in the middle of the place.

Sam used his torch as he moved among the crates reading names and addresses. Nearly every box or bale was from some Eastern Seaboard location. There were a few from the Middle West or the Far West, but what Sam noticed in particular was that none of the boxes had overseas markings, either European or Oriental.

Cohn had indicated that his company did very little international business. This group of stencillings tended to bear that out. Cohn had also implied to Sam that Asche and Cohn Associates did some order-buying, that is, took orders for

106

merchandise, then sought it and bought it, for a percentage. There was evidence on Bills of Lading attached to some of the warehoused goods that this too, was true.

Sam switched off his torch and made an hour-long, very careful examination of the warehouse itself, of the office-area, even of the truck-bed-high outer docks, belted in bruised, thick steel, where great trucks backed up un-gently to unload, or perhaps take on loads.

The front dock was small, divided by the high, very wide sliding doors that permitted trucks to enter the warehouse. The rear dock, just as massively constructed, girded with that steel-plate reinforcement in every area where a truck could back into it, was a little higher off the ground.

Otherwise, to the north and south, the old building had high, weathered, badly warped and hastily patched wooden walls. It wouldn't have been possible, especially at night, to properly surmise the age of the warehouse, but the south driveway between the Asche and Cohn building and an adjoining, equally as disreputable structure, although covered with layers of macadam, still showed on both edges, close to the buildings, that cobblestones were beneath the later layers of paving and oiling.

Sam had some idea of the age of the neighbourhood. He'd once read a book on the entire Manhattan Island area put out by some civic historical association. Once, there had been dray teams and huge wagons moving through the gas-light of this area day and night. But that had been long ago. When ocean-going ships of the present enormous size had required better berthing, this particular area had been abandoned in favour of the more compatible harbours existing elsewhere.

A huge rat with torn ears ran up, halted and reared up on its haunches to squint at Sam. It made an unpleasant chittering sound which could have been a challenge or a warning, Sam had no idea, then it dropped back down on to all fours and scampered away.

Apparently some descendants of the

earlier inhabitants of this derelict area declined to move.

Sam lit a cigarette and stood on the back dock of the warehouse making a slow study of the other delapidated buildings round about. He did not use the torch again, and his chittering old ragged-eared associate did not return.

Later, going down the stairs off the rear dock, Sam put out his smoke and walked without haste in the direction of the abandoned old warehouse not too distant where Franz Ludwig had died.

There was a distant rumbling to prove the city was very much alive elsewhere, but the only sound Sam heard as he walked the gritty old sidewalk was an echo of his own footfalls.

Now and then he saw huddled skeletons in recessed doorways stir at his passing. He paid them very little heed. Once too, he saw the amber light atop a prowl-car cross an intersection far ahead and disappear beyond the next tier of ghostly buildings.

Then he reached the doorless, window-less old hulk of a rotting warehouse where Sauerkraut had died, and entered through a floor-to-ceiling window, where no glass, not even slivers, had existed for perhaps as many years as Sam Adams was old.

He knew where the derelicts would be, if, in fact, they were still using this building; far enough back so that they could see the street, out where sickly lamps gave off milky light, but where they could not, in turn, be seen, themselves. It was their instinctive, defensive mechanism. Even if other alcoholics saw them crouching in there, or if the cruising prowl-cars saw them, they'd be safe. Neither of the others would be particularly threatening.

Sam found them, four ghosts sitting on old crates with newspapers wrapped round their legs to keep out the cold, totally oblivious to Sam, to everything, in fact, except some vague urge that drove them to huddle against one another.

Sam lit a cigarette, more because he preferred the smell of smoke than because he felt any need for tobacco. He spoke gently, looming huge above them. They didn't so much as raise a head, utter a sound, open an eye that couldn't have properly focused anyway. He blew smoke, turned and stepped across where the chalk outline was barely discernible now, stood considering the shadowy outline of death on that ancient, rotting plank floor then ambled farther back through this other old derelict building.

Refuse was everywhere. He was driven to employ his torch a time or two where otherwise he'd surely have stumbled. Finally, he had come full circle; those fluttery shapes were in front of him again, still quite oblivious. He watched as they moved their lips occasionally, or gestured weakly with a hand. They were past pity, past understanding which has to be the basis of pity. He turned in disgust and started away, and one of them, perhaps alerted by the sound of a large man moving through gritty filth, gave a sudden lurch of alarm and cried out a name. Another man, brought instantly alert, began throwing his arms around and cursing.

Sam kept right on moving ahead until

he'd stepped through the windowless opening onto the sidewalk. There, he turned to look back. The wraiths were all still again, silent and hunched and oblivious.

Sam threw away his cigarette, started back where he'd left the sedan, and was caught very suddenly by a blinding flash of steady light from the side of a police car.

The cruiser came alongside, switched off its light and two men climbed out. They were not the same patrolmen Sam had met before, but all that signified was that it had to be past midnight and the shift had changed again.

He identified himself, heard himself being checked-out on the intercom by the policeman who remained on the far side of the prowl-car, then the smooth-faced rookie who had stepped in front of Sam handed back the I.D. folder and grinned.

'You looked pretty damned healthy to be a native,' he said. 'Are you looking for some particular one of 'em?'

'I'm looking,' said Sam, tucking away

the folder, 'for a bolt of brocade cloth.'

The patrolmen looked at Sam as though he'd just said black was really white. The smooth-faced good-natured one repeated that. 'A bolt of brocade cloth. Wait a minute; wasn't that what got stolen out of the warehouse over on the docks a week or so back; brocade and silk?'

'The same,' said Sam, and looked at his watch.

The smooth-faced young patrolman shook his head. 'What makes you think it's around here?'

'Were either of you familiar with the one they called Sauerkraut?'

'No. But then we can't begin to catalogue them all. This Sauerkraut got shot.'

'Another one got shot too.'

'We just heard about that. Charley; we knew him. I guess just about everyone knew Charley. He was a troublesome little — '

'I think Charley might have known where Sauerkraut carried a bolt of brocade cloth, and dropped it. I also believe Sauerkraut didn't remember the cloth at all, and had no idea where he'd left it. So — he got shot. Well; if he'd remembered and had given it up, he'd have got shot just the same.'

'What's so wonderful about a bolt of brocade cloth?' asked the young policeman.

'Heroin,' explained Sam, but that was all he said; he didn't attempt to explain that the heroin was *in* the cloth. 'If you knew Charley, maybe you'd have some idea where he and Sauerkraut circulated.'

The heretofore silent patrolman pointed to the warehouse Sam had recently come out of. 'Over there. But you've been through that place. That's what brought us over — your torch.'

'Where else?' asked Sam, and both officers looked at one another, then shook their heads. They didn't keep close watch on the skeletons, they said. Moreover, the wraiths did not always remain with one group. Sometimes they'd decide, for whatever reason seemed reasonable to them, that they liked another tribe better,

114

or preferred a different old building.

'It's a needle in a haystack,' said the smooth-faced officer, 'trying to find out anything down here. I've often said this is probably the only place on earth where a guy with a polygraph could be driven crazy. You could give 'em lie-detector tests day in and day out, and never get a single jump of the needle. As for a bolt of cloth . . . ' The man shook his head slowly and emphatically from side to side.

Sam didn't quite agree. At least he didn't agree that finding the bolt of cloth would be impossible. His reason was elemental; whether Sauerkraut remembered taking the bolt with him after tearing off a piece for a handkerchief, or whether Charley remembered him doing that, wasn't the issue. What *was* important was Sam's knowledge that, as physically debilitated as these men were, Sauerkraut couldn't have carried the bolt very far. Even if he'd wanted to, even if he remembered why he was lugging the cloth around with him, which he wouldn't remember ten minutes after staggering out of the Asche and Cohn warehouse with it, he still wouldn't have had the physical strength to carry it very far.

That was what Sam had been doing since he'd got rid of Helen; trying to re-trace the route Sauerkraut might have taken, and discover a bolt of Oriental brocade lying somewhere along the way.

If it had been dropped in the gutter, undoubtedly someone else had come along and picked it up. But Sam was reasonably certain of one thing. The heroin-importers who had stolen the other bolts of impregnated cloth weren't the ones who'd found the bolt in a gutter, although someone — perhaps Charley again — had told them who it was that had taken the cloth. If *they'd* found the cloth, why had they come back several times to take Sauerkraut to one side and ask him a lot of questions?

'Tell you what,' said the smooth-faced patrolman. 'We'll keep our eyes peeled. And we'll pass the word along to the other units. Okay?'

Sam smiled. 'Okay. Thanks fellow. Good night.'

He walked away leaving the patrolmen gazing after him as though they had serious misgivings about Sam's mental balance.

He might have reacted in the same way had he been in their boots, but he wasn't in their boots. By the time he got back to his sedan and looked at his wrist again, it was past one o'clock in the morning. One of the forlorn aspects of detective work was that there was no such thing as overtime pay.

He drove to his flat, left the car outside, stamped up to his rooms and went rummaging in the refrigerator for a cold can of beer. This he drank while standing in front of a grimy window, then he shed his clothes, took a hot shower and climbed into bed.

There were plenty of times when being a detective just was not rewarding at all. This was one of them.

10

Tantalising Hints

Helen was discreet, upon occasion. When Sam came ambling in the following morning looking less than bright-eyed and bushy-tailed, she did not ask where he'd gone or what he'd done after taking her home, although judging from appearance he certainly hadn't gone straight home, as she had every right to assume he would have done.

She had the copy of a teletype to show him. The Hong Kong authorities were interested in that tale of impregnating cloth with heroin. They were sceptical too, although they did not specifically say so; it was evident in the way they worded their reply. They did, however, have one little gem to drop before Sam Adams. The name of a man known to them as Robert Borzoi, a US citizen, they claimed, although he'd been born in Shanghai. An eurasian whose multiple talents included just about every phase of smuggling, and mayhem as well, although the latter had never been successfully proved.

Sam asked Helen to query the immigration authorities about the name Robert Borzoi, then hiked down to the files rooms to inaugurate a search of his own. He did not anticipate much success, which was fortunate, because he had none.

Helen did. When he returned to the office a little after eleven o'clock, she had the information on her dictation tablet. 'That really is his name, but he also has a half dozen aliases. They are — '

'Later. What else did they have to say about him?'

'He was under indictment two years ago as an undesirable alien, but he disappeared and they haven't run across him since. Also, he probably has connections in Mainland China, because they have evidence that when he's disappeared on other occasions, that's where he goes.'

'And the smuggling?'

'Dope. The immigration people once banned an associate of his, an Indian from Madras, coming into the country on a diplomatic visa, with a suitcase full of the pure stuff. They had to let the Indian go because of that diplomatic status, but before they released the man he told them the dope actually belonged to a man named Robert Borzoi.'

Sam smiled, lit a cigarette, leaned back in the chair beside Helen's desk and said softly, 'You're a wizard, Curly-head. I don't know what I'd do without you.'

Helen dropped her eyes demurely as she replied. 'We could pursue that over supper at my place this evening, Sam.'

He rose, picked up the list of names she'd written in longhand, and started for the door. 'They've got to have something on Mister Borzoi under one of these aliases downstairs. If anyone wants me you know where I'll be.'

He'd barely closed the door before she said, 'I also know where I'd like to send you right this minute!'

One of the aliases of Robert Borzoi was Robert Bronson, and Sam's hunch was good, there was a rap-sheet on one Robert Bronson, whose vital statistics included a brusque sentence stating that Bronson had a very faint lisping, faintly sing-song accent.

Sam read the rap-sheet while standing near a sunlighted window. It listed several apprehensions but only one legitimate booking, and that had been almost three years earlier when Borzoi-Bronson had been picked up for drunk-driving, for which he'd been sentenced to a stiff fine, had paid and had not been picked up since, although there was a code number at the bottom of the record indicating he also had a Federal record.

What Sam sought was not there; the addresses of apartments, the names of Probation Officers, the list of places where Borzoi might be found.

He returned to the office and Helen smiled sweetly when he asked her to telephone the immigration people again, as well as the local FBI office for whatever they had that might be current enough to help Sam locate his man.

She handed him a note. The plain

clothes man assigned to Jonas at the hospital reported that his ward was proving difficult; Jonas did not want to remain in protective custody. Sam nodded about that and, without a second thought, told Helen when the officer called in, she was to tell him there was no longer any need for him to act as Jonas's bodyguard.

He went into his private office with the report from Hong Kong. The wording was cordial but different; the dictating officer seemed to Sam to be remaining aloof of this business of impregnating cloth with heroin. Even though the message implied interest, candid curiosity over the process employed, it also seemed to convey to Sam a good deal of scepticism. But, and this was what Sam was concerned with, there was a definite statement that a quiet investigation would be undertaken at once.

The reason Sam felt rather keenly about this was elemental; if Borzoi, or someone else, had finally hit upon a practically detection-proof method of getting dangerous drugs into the country, it could only be a matter of time before every bit of cloth coming in would have to be subjected to rigorous tests, and that would without doubt cause a great hue and cry.

Inevitably, skilled people would devise means for simple detection as they had for just about every other ingenious scheme for smuggling dope in, but during the interim an awful lot of the stuff could reach American dope-merchants undetected. *That* was where the peril lay.

Helen appeared in the office doorway. 'The immigration records have no addresses later than two years ago, Sam.'

'That's encouraging. How about the FBI?'

'Yes. I've copied down the addresses they gave me. Incidentally, they've had Mister Borzoi under surveillance for the past year at the request of the CIA.' As Sam's thick brows shot up, Helen said, 'Isn't that fascinating; there seems to be some reason to believe Mister Borzoi might be a courier between the

Communist Chinese and their agents in South America. He flies to Mexico City rather frequently. In fact, the best address they have for him is down there. It's only a month old.'

Sam left his desk, came round it and reached for the slip of paper Helen held forth. 'I have a very good friend in Mexico City,' he said, studying the piece of paper. 'I'll use your telephone, then you can take down what's said.'

He had reached the chair beside her desk in the outer office, had his hand extended towards the telephone, when Lieutenant Stokes walked in looking, as he usually did, mildly dissatisfied about something.

Sam nodded a silent greeting, kept his hand poised to swoop downward, and waited. Lieutenant Stokes, a man impressed with his importance as second-in-command of detectives, paced across the little room, nodded gravely at Helen, then said, 'I picked up something that might help a little in the Franz Ludwig thing, Sam.'

While Stokes paused, Sam reluctantly

drew his hand back, squared around in the chair and waited stoically. He was very seldom in a hurry about anything, but there was invariably one point in every assignment where excitement appeared; in his current assignment this was that point.

'A query came in a few minutes ago regarding some white brocade cloth.'

Sam stiffened in the chair. Over by the doorway Helen also seemed suddenly to become intensely alert. Stokes smiled benignly at them both.

'I recalled something that was said about Ludwig having a brocade handkerchief, which was somehow significant in his case. That's why I came round.'

Sam said, 'Where is this cloth, Lieutenant?'

'Downstairs in the laboratory, I believe.'

'Who found it?'

'Well, it wasn't found, exactly. Some officers working the garment district heard about a woman known as a pilferer trying to sell some white brocade, still in the bolt. They rounded her up, with the cloth. They had to turn her loose, but she gave them the cloth, and they sent out feelers, thinking that the cloth had to have been stolen.'

Sam rose. 'Good. I'll go down to the lab. Lieutenant, I'll appreciate it if you'll ask those patrolmen to come to my office as soon as possible.'

Stokes beamed. It was easy to see he'd just handed Detective Adams a valuable bit of information, and of course that insured that in the final disposition of Sam's present assignment, it would be mentioned that Lieutenant Stokes had helped. It had never been known to be a cause of injury to an ambitious man's record that he was alert and helpful in a crisis.

After Stokes had departed Helen said, 'Sam, while you're gone do you suppose I ought to contact those patrolmen for the name and address of that woman they got the brocade from?'

'Do that,' he said, striding for the door.

He chose the stairs instead of the lift in his swift march to the laboratory, and the moment he saw the bolt of cloth he knew it was the right one. He showed the technician assigned to identifying and classifying the brocade where Franz Ludwig had torn off a piece. He also told the technician if he got that improvised handkerchief, then tested both bits of cloth, he'd find heroin impregnated in each piece.

It proved to be exactly as he said, too, except that the bolt, soiled and rumpled now, yielded up a staggering amount of re-claimable heroin. The technician went to get an associate, an older man whose experience with narcotics was wider, then between them they measured the amount of heroin in the cloth, the amount that could be reclaimed, re-refined into crystals, and came up with a figure that surprised even Sam.

The older technician stood peering at the cloth as he polished his glasses. 'I'm always amazed,' he quietly said, 'at the near-genius of people who do things like this to break the law, when if they'd use the same genius in legitimate fields they'd probably get much richer, and they'd certainly never spend so many years of their lives in prisons. Sam, there is a fortune in what that cloth had in it. I don't mean a small fortune, not just a comfortable fortune, I'm thinking in terms of perhaps a quarter of a million dollars. How many bolts of this cloth came into the country along with this bolt?'

Sam did not have the answer to that, and right at the moment that didn't interest him very much. He left instructions for the re-claimed heroin and the bolt of brocade to be locked up very securely, then he returned to his office, where Helen was getting ready to go to lunch. It was, in fact, half an hour past lunch time.

She handed him one of those little slips of paper taken from her dictation pad. 'The woman's name is Sally Janichek. That's her present address right below the name. I also called down for her rap-sheet. They're sending it up. Sam? You could go to lunch with me. By the time we got back the rap-sheet would be here.'

He shook his head, read the address

over twice then said, 'I'm not hungry. I'll be in contact later.' He then turned and left the office again, and Helen simply gazed after him this time with a forlorn, resigned expression, and didn't have a single word to say.

He drove away from the police building with the noon-day traffic as thick as it ever was. The area he was heading for was definitely not the high-rise district; it was close to the garment section of town, which was a mad, mad world all its own.

By the time he found the brownstone tenement he sought, it was past one o'clock, and by the time he got up the rickety stairs to the third floor, and discovered that the doorbell didn't work and knocked loudly, it was along towards two o'clock.

Sally Janichek peered out of a crack before opening the door, and she assumed an expression of resigned exasperation as she said, 'Cops. I knew it before I even opened the lousy door. Every time I turn round there's cops. Look, how come you guys never catch these stabbers and murderers and whatnot; I'll tell you why — because you're always hecklin' poor old women like me who are only trying to live. That's all. Just trying to — '

'May I come in?' asked Sam, already leaning slightly against the old woman's relaxing pressure upon the panel that separated them.

'Can you? Would it do me any good to say no you can't? Listen, let me tell you something, Lieutenant: They always pick big guys for roughing up little old women, don't they? And for why, I'd like to know? All I did was find this dirty bolt of cloth, which someone had flung away, obviously, and all I done then was take it round trying to get maybe five dollars for it. And the cops grab me. Can you come in? Well, damn it all, you're already in, aren't you? All right; you can sit on the cot. I'll stand right here. All right; now what is it this time — you going to hit me or something?'

11

Routine Revelations

Sam plucked ten dollars from his wallet and put them upon a littered and filthy dresser. 'That's for the bolt of cloth,' he explained. 'Your asking price for the bolt was five, that is ten. Okay?'

The horribly made-up old face peered dresser-wards as though suspecting some kind of trap. 'Cops don't do people favours. How come ten dollars?'

Sam smiled. 'Sally, I'm buying bolts of soiled brocade today. Tomorrow it may not be cloth at all. You just got lucky today.'

'I can imagine,' sniffed the old thief. She moved closer to the littered, un-made cot which was obviously her bed, since there was only one room to her living quarters. She flung a few items aside and perched on the cot's edge looking upwards.

'Okay, fuzz,' she said. 'Now hit me.'

Sam almost laughed and his humour infected the old woman a little. At least her ratty little darting eyes lit up faintly.

'All right, then you aren't going to hit me. What then? Look, I'm sixty. You wouldn't be interested in — '

'Information,' said Sam. 'Where did you get the brocade, Sally?'

'Under the docks down by a warehouse.'

'What warehouse?'

'How should I know? An old one though, with rats as big as cats. There is an old dock south of there a block or so. I was comin' down the alleyway from behind that warehouse heading towards the old docks. Sometimes you can find stuff down there.'

'Was the cloth actually *under* the dock, Sally?'

'Under it, Cop. I seen something white through a crack in the planking, so I went down there. The cloth was lying right where somebody tossed it. It hadn't been there too long either, because the mud hadn't soaked all the way through.'

'Who put it under there, Sally?'

'F'gawdsake, who do you think I am? The FBI that I go round spying on people? I got no idea at all who put the cloth under there. Maybe some wino. Maybe somebody stole the stuff and flung it under there meaning to come back. Maybe anything. All I know is that I saw the white shine of the cloth through the dock planking. I went down one of those old ladders, found the stuff, then took it out and tried to peddle it. Then the cops came and you know the rest.'

Sam made her draw him a rough diagram of exactly where she'd found the cloth. He was satisfied she'd told the truth when she'd said she didn't know who'd put the brocade under the dock, and he was also satisfied that no one had seen her remove it who had any interest in the cloth. If someone like that *had* seen her removing the brocade she'd be lying dead under the docks herself.

He could of course have taken her with him to the spot where the cloth had been found. He didn't because he knew he'd find the place, and furthermore he didn't want to have to bring her back, nor, for the matter of that, sit in the same car with her for very long.

Before taking his leave he also speculated on her safety. She would be safe enough as long as Bronson-Borzoi did not know she was the one who had found the bolt of cloth. He also speculated on the possibility of locating Borzoi and arresting him before he knew anyone at all had found his precious brocade.

On the drive to the warehouse area he tried to imagine why Franz Ludwig had gone in that direction; it was directly opposite to the direction he'd have travelled to reach his tribal warehouse.

It was very probable that, now, Sam Adams would never know why this had been done. Apart from Ludwig's passing, the only other believable source of personal information respecting Ludwig was also dead — Charley.

Not that it mattered terribly, except that Sam would have been interested in having some kind of an answer.

He parked within rifle-shot of the

Asche and Cohn building, paused to light a cigarette and consider the plausible course Ludwig had taken, then turned and sauntered along to the docks where a normally pleasant little breeze was now carrying along the accumulated stenches of miles of riverfront garbage and other assorted refuse.

The area hereabouts was scabrous as well as odoriferous. An occasional set of stairs leading down to the waterline appeared to tempt Sam, but he chose the one he used with some care. The others were so rotten they'd have collapsed under his formidable weight.

He found the spot where fresh tracks indicated the only recent two-legged visitor in ages had come along, but it told him nothing except that the bolt of cloth had been lying here and that someone wearing women's shoes, Sally Janichek undoubtedly, had lifted the bolt and had scuttled triumphantly up a nearby set of those deadly old steps.

He finished his smoke down there, flicked it into the oily mud and went back up on to the dock to stand and make another study of the probable course Franz Ludwig had taken.

He was satisfied that the circumstantial evidence of everything that had occurred was correct. He did not have to prove any of it, which was probably very fortunate, so as he slid back into the car to head back for the office he was feeling satisfied.

Time, he discovered when he reached the office, was an ally only of people who worked from nine-to-five. Helen, for example, was gone, the cover was on her typewriter, and his watch told him that it was indeed past quitting time.

Regardless, he went on through to his private office where messages would be left on the desk, if there were any.

There were. One giving the Mexico City address of Robert Bronson. Sam smiled over that; he had no idea by what ruse Helen had managed to procure that address, but he had never under-estimated her capabilities either. It would be authentic.

The second note was also interesting. That plain clothes man Sam had put to keeping an eye on Pierre O'Gorman had reported-in that the shipping clerk, a man named Howard Wax, from the Asche and Cohn warehouse had gone round to O'Gorman's saloon shortly after lunch time, had a beer, had a little conversation with O'Gorman, then had returned to work at the warehouse.

Sam responded to each not in proper order. He teletyped a request to the FBI for whatever address anyone had on Bronson-Borzoi subsequent to the Mexico City number. He requested immediate action and an urgent reply.

He then telephoned the clerk of the local unit of the Warehousemen and Dock-Workers International Brotherhood, got the address of one Howard Wax, and armed with these two things, a name and an address, he dropped downstairs to make a file search.

Howard Wax, it came to light, was a probationer. He'd been with Asche and Cohn one year. Prior to that he'd been steadily employed in the clerical department of State Prison for four years upon the recommendation of a jury which had found him guilty of extortion.

There were two other former felonies, one, felonious assault, the other complicity with others in smuggling.

Sam returned to his office, lit a cigarette, saw a magazine Helen had left in his mail-basket, saw the pointedly face-up, bold-type proclaiming the insidious evils of tobacco-smoking, took down a very pleasant big lungful, turned the magazine face-down, and propped both feet on the desk. Things at long last seemed to be moving along. As soon as the FBI teletype came in he'd lock up the store for the night.

Meanwhile, he'd sit and smoke and gloat a little. Every detective was entitled to one good gloat per case. In fact, without a genuine gloat now and then the entire business would be appallingly disgusting.

Howard Wax was undoubtedly the contact-man for the heroin importers. Otherwise, after a two-month delay, how could they have known precisely when to burglarize the Asche and Cohn

Warehouse and retrieve the cloth.

On the other end, of course, there had to be someone like Howard Wax to flash the word when the brocade and silk were to be loaded and forwarded. That would be the responsibility of the Hong Kong authorities.

There were some other aspects that Her Majesty's lads in their knee-breeches could also sweat-out. For example, how did the people in Hong Kong know to ship to Asche and Cohn, providing of course neither Mister Asche nor Mister Cohn were involved, and how did Howard Wax get his employers to order the brocade and silk? It might pay to have the West Coast authorities look into Hyman and Company, for whom that cloth had been ordered.

The telephone rang. The brisk if boyish voice of the night-man down in Communications reported an answer was coming in to Sam's FBI query. Sam rang off, arose and with a little mock bow in the direction of Washington, said aloud, 'Thank you, oh great and benevolent J. Edgar.'

The corridor outside was empty. Sam's footfalls sounded unusually loud upon the cement as he trotted down stairs. His telephone was ringing but he didn't know that since he'd closed the outer door of the office.

His reply from the Federal Bureau of Investigation was succinct. It simply gave a Manhattan address, adding that this was reportedly a delicatessen store, and that if there were no living quarters above it or in back of it, then it was probably a 'drop', or contact-point, for Robert Borzoi.

No mention was made of Borzoi's FBI record, or of how this latest address had been discovered. Sam took the message with him and struck out for the parked sedan outside. It was getting dark now and he was hungry. He was also mildly sardonic; although Federal Bureau of Investigation co-operation with municipal police departments was usually good, prompt, and accurately informative, there was an aloofness that put Sam in mind of a hinted similar aloofness on the part of those gentlemen in Hong Kong who had been exchanging communications with him via teletype.

He could guess where the FBI had got that latest address: the CIA. But wild horses wouldn't have forced them to divulge this.

Sam slid into the car, gunned the motor and eased out of his parking slot. It was perfectly agreeable with him if the federal agencies wanted to play cops-and-robbers. All he wanted was a triggerman.

When he reached his flat and started shedding clothing on his way to the shower, the telephone rang. It was Helen. She said she'd tried contacting him at the office and hadn't been able to raise anyone. He explained that he'd been in the office only long enough to read her notes then start acting upon them.

She said, 'It's almost eight o'clock, Sam. Can't you turn it off now, the taxpayers have got their money's worth for today.'

He nodded at the wall. 'Sure.'

'Well, I picked up two beautiful T-bone steaks on my way home this evening. I've got the fire just right to drop them in. How long will it take you to get over here? And I've got a bottle of *sake*.'

'*Sake?* What's the occasion?'

'A third note. One I didn't leave on your desk.'

He pondered. He was perfectly willing to go over and eat one of her steaks, after he'd cleaned up of course, but the idea of being mildly blackmailed didn't strike him very benevolently at the moment. It had been another long and trying day. Furthermore, he was put-out. Pierre O'Gorman had in all probability lied to him about knowing Franz Ludwig, or anything Ludwig was involved in. It always upset Sam a little to discover he'd been lied to.

'Well?' she said. 'Are you coming or aren't you?'

'I'm coming.'

'How long will you be?'

'How long does it take to broil a steak?'

'Depends. You like your meat well-done. Perhaps ten or twelve minutes.'

'I can't make it that fast, I've got

to shower and change. Allow a half hour. And I resent having you withhold information.'

'For your own good, Sam. If you don't agree when you get here, you can spank me.'

'Odd you should mention that. I was toying with the idea.'

'I'm speaking in the figurative sense, Sam.'

'I'm not,' he said, and put down the telephone, rose with a grunt and went ahead preparing for the shower he'd have taken in any event. Also, now that his salivary glands had been titillated, he began feeling more hungry than ever.

And of course he was curious about this big secret Helen had that was so critical she couldn't leave it in note-form on his desk.

12

A Positive Identification!

She'd been burning incense. When he walked in, the little apartment smelled wonderfully conglomerate. She brought him a glass of the rice wine, beamed at him and said, 'You don't look worn out.'

'That's nice.' He tasted the *sake*, found it palatable and went to a chair to sit and finish it. 'What's the big secret? And that reminds me . . . '

She stood looking down at him. 'If you lay a hand on me I'll scream, and there is a big burly wrestler who lives next door.'

'Okay. I'm not up to that tonight. What's the secret?'

She had to go and check on the steaks. He watched her depart, thought of trailing after, then gave in to an urge to simply sit and sip *sake*.

She called him a few moments later. As he rose she whisked away the tiny apron she'd been wearing and went to stand by her place at the table watching his reaction to the steak on his plate. He showed appreciation with a smile. As they sat, he told her incense and steak-aroma actually made a very interesting scent.

She looked dubious, as though she suspected him of making fun of her in a dead-pan way.

'The secret isn't really a secret, but it's something I hesitated about leaving on your desk.'

'This steak,' he announced, 'is perfect. You're a good cook, Curly-head.'

'Lieutenant Stokes put two men among the winos this afternoon, and one of them has already reported back that there is one group in the area of O'Gorman's tavern that aren't really winos at all.'

Sam stopped his moving fork. 'Ahhhh?'

'Lieutenant Stokes wanted you to know that this afternoon, but I couldn't locate you. He wants you to contact one of the undercover men for details.'

Sam resumed eating and very slowly dark colour began mounting up from his throat into his face. Eventually he said,

'You could have left that in a note on the desk. And what does Stokes think he's doing, jumping into my case?'

'Sam, he's lieutenant of detectives.'

'I wonder how he'd like a punch in the nose.'

'Sam Adams!

'Look, I've got the name of the man I'm sure killed Ludwig. You helped with the address, but I got a better one, right here in Manhattan. Also, I know about the bolt of brocade. In fact, what has Stokes done, except turn up one little fact — the cloth — which would have come through the bureaux in routine fashion anyway. But now, all of a sudden, he's got to climb aboard the gravy-train. I think I'll tell him all this first thing in the morning!'

'For heaven's sake, Sam, we all work together, don't we?'

'Oh yeah? Well, where was Old Ironsides when I was first handed this mess?'

'You're acting like a child. And you're being ridiculous. Lieutenant Stokes simply wants to see justice done.'

'Cut it out! Justice doesn't enter into it. It never does. Not with Stokes, not with me, not with Chief Hall, and not with you. We're cops, pure and simple. That justice-stuff doesn't filter down to us. That's for the judges and attorneys and jurymen to fret about.'

'I'll get you more coffee. Is the steak really good?'

'Wonderful. And furthermore, with any luck I'll wrap it up tomorrow. If I can nab Borzoi at the address the FBI furnished me.'

'Wrap it up? Sam, you don't have enough to wrap it up. You don't even have a witness.'

He leaned back for her to re-fill his cup, scowled and said, 'The more I think about it, the better it sounds.'

'What?'

'Punching Stokes in the nose.'

'Sam Adams you're wearing out my patience. I shouldn't have told you to meet Lieutenant Stokes's man down near O'Gorman's saloon.'

Sam's indignation, and it was actually never more than that, withered as he ate

147

and drank and got torpidly comfortable. He finally was down to unpleasant little grunts, out on the sofa in Helen's small sitting-room, and she was no longer feeding the fire of his annoyance with remonstrances. Instead, she was telling him about the young man named Garfunckel who was showing definite interest in Margery Fein, Lieutenant Stokes's secretary.

He couldn't possibly have been interested. For one thing he was now becoming more and more certain about O'Gorman's involvement with Borzoi. For another, he was speculating on what had happened to the other bolts of that impregnated Oriental cloth. Every federal and state agency had a narcotics bureau. Somewhere along the line one of those departments was going to come up with a statistic concerning increased sales in some particular locality. He had to know where that area was, when this happened, and he had to be able to tie in his own felons.

Finally, shortly before he left Helen's flat, he said, 'What time am I to meet Stokes's man?'

'Ten o'clock in the morning, Sam. He'll be watching for you down along the docks across from the Asche and Cohn warehouse. And Sam — please . . . ?'

He smiled. 'You know I'm always indefatigably cheerful at ten o'clock in the morning, Curly-head. Well, it's been a wonderful evening. You can cook steaks better than my mother could.'

'I also iron well, Sam, and — '

'I won't be in the office first thing, so if Stokes comes around panting for his share of fame, just say I'll contact him when I do get in.'

He kissed her cheek, which he did not ordinarily do, but then it was warm in the apartment, and *sake* always loosened inhibitions best in warm rooms, then he departed.

By the time he got home it was midnight and he was in a kind of benevolent stupor. He was also dog-tired; this wasn't the first night he'd missed his sleep lately.

The ensuing morning he was stirring by six, out of the flat by seven, and down in the skid-row neighbourhood by eight o'clock, which was a horrible hour to visit that derelict-ridden part of the city. The sun, which never quite reached some of the nooks and crannies, didn't brighten the grey, wretched world around O'Gorman's tavern until after nine. O'Gorman, however, opened his place by eight; not because he anticipated customers but because, living as he did in a waterless room nearby, the only place he could shave and fry breakfast was in the roach-infested cubbyhole-kitchen off the bar.

No one was inside when Sam entered quietly, took a position astride a bar-stool and slammed a great fist down on the bar. At once an angry, withered, sly-eyed face sprang from round the kitchen-door and a howl of profane indignation was half started before O'Gorman recognized his patron. He swallowed with an effort and continued to glower as he came on into the bar-room.

'You an insomniac or something?' he demanded.

Sam sat and glowered right back. 'That's better than being a lousy liar.'

O'Gorman shuffled his feet, picked up a rag and wiped his hands on it, then tossed it down again. 'Me . . . ?'

'You. What was it you said — you didn't know Sauerkraut?'

'I told you, damn it all, that I didn't *remember* him. They come and they go. Yesterday there's this other guy came around asking questions too. I told him the same thing. Sauerkraut was just a — '

'Wait a minute. What other guy?'

'How do I know? He's never been in here before. He wasn't a wino, and that's how I know he'd never been around before.'

'What did he want to know?'

'If Sauerkraut ever left things for me to keep for him.'

Sam fished forth his cigarettes, offered O'Gorman one, which was accepted, then flicked his lighter for them both. 'This stranger didn't give his name, of course.'

'Of course.'

'But you'd know him if you saw him again.'

'Of course. My eggs are burning!'

O'Gorman fled, cursing, back into his little kitchen where the violence of his profanity rose to a hair-raising crescendo, then subsided and moments later, when he returned, he was more angry than before.

'You owe me for two burnt eggs!'

Sam fished out a paper dollar, smoothed it out and genially smiled. 'For the eggs. Now listen, I want you to take a little ride with me and look at a man.'

'I run a business. I can't just lock up and go look at picture books because — '

'You're not going to look at pictures, and you won't have a wino in here until noon. Get your hat.'

'I don't wear a hat.'

'Then take off that damned apron,' said Sam, stepping back from the bar.

O'Gorman flung the apron upon the bar with great indignation, but he obeyed. As they were getting into Sam's sedan he said, 'You'll owe me for the time, too.'

Sam sighed, wheeled away from the dirty kerbing and drove in stolid silence down to the Asche and Cohn warehouse. He parked some little distance away, pointed to the building and said, 'Sit in the car and watch the doors over there. I'll go inside and parade a man out front on the loading dock. You take a real good look at him.'

'What for,' grumbled O'Gorman, pointing. 'That's the guy, standing there with that truck-driver, with the clipboard in his hand. The one that just come out.'

Sam swung heavily to see in the opposite direction. He had never seen Howard Wax himself, and in fact when he'd stopped his car that truck had just been turning into the warehouse's front entrance.

Howard Wax was a slight man; this was accentuated now because the trucker he was talking to was a muscle-bound, swarthy man at least six feet tall. Wax looked exactly like a warehouse clerk should look. Sam sighed, straightened back and said, 'Would you be able to swear to that in court?'

O'Gorman shifted his attention from the pair of men on the distant dock, to Sam Adams. He considered his reply carefully and Sam could almost have quoted his precise words before O'Gorman uttered them.

'Who pays me for my time? After all, I make little enough pouring wine for bums, but taking time off for court appearances.'

'You'll be paid,' said Sam, unpleasantly, and started the car. 'Are you sure that's the man?'

'I'm as sure as I am of my own name.'

They returned to the tavern and Sam let O'Gorman out at the kerbing with one final word. 'Pierre; if this bird comes around again, be very careful.'

O'Gorman squinted his disillusioned, sulky eyes.

'As a result of some kind of hanky-panky two guys have been killed, and you think you got to tell *me* to be careful!'

Sam grinned although it was difficult for him to really like Pierre O'Gorman. To the barman people were pigs. Justified or not, in view of O'Gorman's environment, it didn't sit very well with Sam, who, although not a totally compassionate person himself, nonetheless did not blanket all humanity in his dislikes.

He considered the element of time and decided that he wouldn't be able to meet Stokes's man without moving fast. As he drove away from O'Gorman's place it was in the back of his mind to telephone to Stokes saying he'd not be able to get back to skid-row by ten o'clock.

In the end, though, he didn't do that.

He drove back up into the bustling heart of Manhattan searching for the delicatessen store whose address he had, and when ultimately he found the place and lingered across the road studying it, there seemed slight evidence, at least from external appearances, that the little store could be a 'front' for someone engaged in high-power illegality.

Satisfied he could find the place without delay when he had to return, he then cruised back down for the meeting with Stokes's man.

It was a little past ten by the time he spotted a dirty, unkempt wino watching him approach on the street passing the Asche and Cohn warehouse. Without any hesitation he headed for a side street nearby, left the car and started to walk back. The wino came round a corner, threw him a beckoning signal and went ambling down in the direction of the same dock where Sam had found the place that bolt of brocade had been lost — and retrieved.

He didn't know the undercover officer, but that was no cause for anxiety; there were hundreds of detectives in the Manhattan community he'd never seen. In the greater New York City area there were thousands of them he'd never met before.

13

The End Envisioned

The plain clothes man identified himself, then jumped right into his story. 'There are four men posing as winos and living in an old tenement about a mile west of here. I called Lieutenant Stokes for an undercover photographer, and I think he got them all yesterday afternoon. Maybe it's nothing, but on the other hand — '

'All right,' said Sam, impatiently. 'What are they up to?'

'As far as I know this minute, nothing. But they aren't alcoholics, I can tell you that.'

'How did you happen to spot them?'

'A new, black car pulled to the kerbing yesterday morning and a fancy-dresser leaned out and tossed something in a bundle to one of them. He tossed something into the car and the driver beat it.'

Sam smiled. 'Very good. Very good indeed. Okay, lie around today and keep an eye on these lands. I'll go and check on the photographer, and if he's got anything we can match to mug-shots I'll have Lieutenant Stokes get in touch with you. By the way, I understood there was another man staked out down here.'

'There is, he's over covering the area where that drunk got shot to death.'

Sam pondered that a moment. Unless his arithmetic was faulty that meant there had to be *two* undercover men in the area of O'Gorman's tavern. And that was foolish. More than foolish, it was very risky. He didn't say any of this to the wino-detective, but when he was on his way back to the office he decided to say it to Lieutenant Stokes.

There was a delay, which just may have been for the good; when he reached the office it was lunchtime and Miss Fein told Sam at the doorway that her boss had gone to eat and wouldn't return for a full hour.

Sam went on along to see what Helen had. Her smile was welcome but her report was not. 'There was an FBI man here earlier, Sam, and a gentleman from the Federal Narcotics Agency. They both said they'd be back.'

She looked pointedly at her wrist. 'You could take me to lunch.'

'Later,' he muttered absently, and went down to the photographic laboratory to see if Stokes's man had come up with anything. He had. The developed prints had been taken with a zoom-lens, evidently, for otherwise there would have been no way to get such excellent close-ups without being detected. The photographer had to be very knowledgeable at his work, which pleased Sam.

He took the four eight-by-ten inch glossy prints to the identification section and started the tedious job of matching faces to names and rap-sheets. There was a comparometer for this, otherwise he could have been down there for several days. Comparometers functioned on a basis of elimination, actually, not on some magic formula that measured skulls, width between eyes, or similar personal characteristics. One of the four nameless men had black curly hair, very dark brown eyes, and a mouth that was pulled slightly to one side as though in a habitual little sneer. These factors did not pinpoint a felon on file, but they *did* eliminate something like five thousand photographed felons who did not have a twisted mouth, dark hair or dark eyes.

It also helped greatly that Sam could get a couple of experienced file searcher to assist in the search. Still, it was past two in the afternoon before they located the man with the sneer. That was definitely encouraging because it permitted them to gain some inkling of this man's associates, and the kind of other felons he was most likely to be working with.

By four o'clock they had located the file on each of the four men, and to Sam's great satisfaction, each felon was known to have an affinity for pushing narcotics.

He took copies of each rap-sheet back upstairs with him, along with the photographs the undercoverman had taken, and when Helen, feeling sorry for him, went downstairs for a ham on rye sandwich and a paper cup of coffee, he was visited by Lieutenant Stokes. But by then Sam was in excellent spirits again. Hungry but smiling.

'You met my man,' said Stokes, taking the only chair in Sam's private cubbyhole not already occupied.

'I met him,' agreed Sam, leaning back to fish round for smokes. 'I've also placed the four fake winos your photographer shot. Narco people, each one.'

'Fine. Anything else?'

'Yeah, one thing. You may be second in command of the detective bureau, Lieutenant, but the next time you jump into a case I'm working on without even letting me know over the telephone you're doing it, I'm going to — '

'Now wait a minute,' broke in Stokes, reddening. 'I have the authority to involve myself in any case at any time.'

Sam's neck turned a blushing pink. 'I'm not questioning that at all, Lieutenant. What I'm squawking about is the way you did it, this time. In case you'd forgotten, there's a nut running around with a gun killing people, in this case, and bollixing things up like you've done could just possibly get someone shot.'

'Sam, I'll be damned if I have to sit here and — !'

'Lieutenant, I'm telling you for the good of both of us. Next time, let me know *before* you jump in with both feet, not after.'

Helen appeared looking worried. As she entered Sam's private office with the paper cup and the sandwich wrapped in transparent paper, she said, 'I could hear you all the way to the lift.' She put the food in front of Sam then gave him a rebuking little frown. 'You said you weren't going to do this, Sam.'

'I didn't say any such a thing, Helen, I said I'd like to — '

'*Sam Adams*!'

The Lieutenant threw up both hands and emitted a loud groan, then dropped his hands. 'Not you too, girl. All right, all right. I'm sorry, Sam. I was at fault. You are exactly right, I should have cleared my movements with you first. I'm sorry and I won't do that again.'

The lieutenant squinted. 'Okay?'

Sam began unwrapping the ham on rye. 'Okay.' He took a big bite, winked at Helen and said, 'You sure can cook, Curly-head.'

She turned in exasperation and walked out of the private office, closing the door on them as she departed.

Lieutenant Stokes watched Sam chew for a moment before attempting to get their conversation back on its original course. Eventually he said, 'Where are we now? You've identified the four fake winos, but have you come up with what they're up to?'

'A guess, pure and simple,' Sam replied. 'Borzoi is the guy with the flashy clothes, the black car, and the lisp, or accent, or whatever it is. He was seen contacting the other four, delivering something to them and picking up something from them.'

'The guess, Sam?'

'The guess is that those four are the people who boil out the heroin, or whatever they do to re-claim it, and I'm also guessing that they do it in some old tenement they inhabit. Also, that when they've re-claimed the crystals they deliver them to Borzoi, who in turn acts as their courier, sells the stuff and brings back money to them.'

'All guesswork?'

Sam nodded. 'Every blessed bit of it. And there's something else. Borzoi has a delicatessen as his front. Maybe he lives on the premises and maybe he simply drops off the kilos of heroin for someone else to take over and re-sell. But I think, if we co-ordinate all our efforts, we ought to be able to bag the lot of them without too much trouble.'

'What about evidence, Sam?'

For a moment there was no reply as Sam downed the coffee, finished the sandwich, then wiped his fingers fastidiously upon a handkerchief.

'There has to be some kind of equipment in that old tenement where those four men re-claim the heroin from the cloth.'

'But the minute we bust in they blow it up or burn the tenement.'

'Then what we've got to do, Lieutenant,

is get inside, verify that the equipment exists, and confiscate it before anyone can wreck it.' Sam lit a cigarette, his last one, crumpled the empty pack in a huge fist and flung it into the deskside wastebasket.

Stokes nodded thoughtfully. He was thinking ahead to the essential evidence the police would have to offer in order to get the District Attorney to agree to prosecute. It never hurt to have all the incriminating evidence one could round up. Stokes asked about witnesses and Sam told him about O'Gorman and Howard Wax.

Stokes eventually stepped to the little window behind Sam and stood looking down into the grimy parking area behind the building. 'The Chief wants to be kept informed,' he said. 'I think you ought to go up and put all the cards on the table for him, Sam.'

The chair squeaked, the floor protested, and Sam's voice didn't sound much better than those other two noises when he answered. 'Don't do me any favours, Lieutenant. *You* go upstairs. I'm a cop,

165

not a politician. You go up there and make it sound very good, and I'll stay down here and try to co-ordinate it.'

Stokes turned, red in the face. 'In case you have forgotten, Sam, I was in this same office doing exactly what you're doing when you first moved up into this bureau. I'm *not* a political cop!'

Sam went to the door and opened it. 'Have it your way, Lieutenant. But I'm the one who is fully familiar with the details. It will work a lot better if I'm also the one who organizes things. And about having *two* undercover men down there — that only compounds the risks of discovery. If I were you I'd call in the lad who is watching O'Gorman.'

'You no longer believe O'Gorman is tied-in?'

'I never said I thought O'Gorman was tied-in, Lieutenant. The worst I'd have said about him was that I thought he'd lied to me. I'm still not so sure he didn't, but at least as far as the lost bolt of cloth is concerned, I'm reasonably sure O'Gorman has no idea about that.'

Lieutenant Stokes took the hint supplied

by the open door and walked out into Helen's office, scowling. He nodded at Sam. 'I'll go upstairs. What are you planning for this afternoon?'

'A personal surveillance of that delicatessen. I want some time to think and that ought to provide it. Also, with any kind of luck, I just might be able to pot Mister Borzoi.'

Stokes went out, Helen turned reproachful eyes on Sam, and he thanked her for the sandwich and coffee. Then, before she could remonstrate, he launched into an explanation of fundamentally everything he had also told Lieutenant Stokes. After a bit it served its purpose, and she forgot to scold him, which was of course the only reason he bothered to give her all those details anyway.

She asked if he intended to wait around for the two federal agents who'd been by earlier to see him. He shook his head. Federal agents, he had the temerity to suggest, could come in second this time, as far as he was concerned, and with a wicked little grin he walked out of the office leaving Helen gazing perplexedly, and a trifle exasperatedly, at the door he'd neglected to close after himself. Next to always forgetting his hat, Sam Adams never, or rarely ever, properly closed a door after he'd passed out of an office.

He considered picking up a Department camera to take along, decided not to and went straight away to his car where the mid-afternoon heat had made the interior as hot as an oven. That didn't much bother him; in fact, he scarcely thought of it at all after inadvertently getting a reminder when he first touched the door.

He left the yard with an impassive expression, turned uptown into the serpentine of late-day traffic and wasn't even very concerned with whether he actually saw Borzoi or not.

His attitude was that of a person upon whom fortune has lavished her bounty to such a degree that he could be a little indifferent.

That was known as gloating. Hot afternoons are the best for gloating, for gloats and gloaters. Sam cruised in the direction of the delicatessen feeling as smug and positive of a quick ending to his current assignment as he'd ever felt.

There was very little reason to believe otherwise, actually. Everyone involved had been identified as to degree of involvement and degree of felonious intent. The exceptions were negligible — Asche and Cohn, primarily, and they couldn't be too involved if indeed they were in any way involved.

Sam came to the neighbourhood of the little delicatessen, saw a parking place — as rare as new money any time of the day — and eased into it, still feeling very confident.

14

Burglary!

In any sector of Manhattan excepting possibly skid-row, and even there it was problematical, a person could by being only slightly discreet, keep an almost indefinite surveillance.

People, like ants, constantly surged one way or another way, and for some reason the neighbourhood, being predominately Jewish, had a bazaar air, a variety of noisy, surging, restless life that absorbed nearly every alien factor, with the little delicatessen in the middle of all that activity, and with Sam Adams across the street and southward a bit, in a coffee shop gazing from the window as customers passed into the delicatessen, emerging later with packages.

Sam was too distant to make out faces and features, but he was in no hurry to get closer. This was his initial reconnoitre. Later, with less sunlight and more human activity, he changed points of vantage, got nearly opposite the delicatessen and from there could distinguish that the people going inside the delicatessen were definitely shoppers. Also, it being later in the day, the rather steady stream picked up a little, in haste as well as in numbers.

He pondered. The delicatessen had a prime location. Its owner did a good business. The entire enterprise was one of those landmark undertakings that throve despite all the calamitous economic events which might rock other neighbourhood business, such as the hearing-aid store adjoining to the north, or even the shoe store to the south.

Of course the proprietor was not going to retire with a fortune, but he would never in his lifetime be financially strapped, nor would he ever be unemployed. How many businesses or businessmen could be assured of those things? Very, very few. So — why would this person, whoever he was, get involved with felons?

It was difficult for Sam Adams to make sense from this. Of course, he had no definite proof that the proprietor *was* actively involved. But it would be difficult for Borzoi to be using that delicatessen as his point of rendezvous with other felons for the disposal of narcotics, without *someone* over there realizing something fishy was going on.

But one thing became evident as time passed: There was no regular meeting of addicts over there, and if narcotics merchants were rendezvousing, they were doing it disguised in a number of very convincing costumes.

Above the store was a typical set of walk-up flats whose soiled old curtains flapped occasionally when a stray breeze came down through the cement canyon. The rooms would be old, wall-papered, inhabited in the way rabbit warrens were inhabited.

It would be relatively simple to locate Borzoi up there. Not very many flashy-dressers would live in this neighbourhood, and a single man owning a shiny black car would stick out like a sore thumb.

Just before the last rusty red rays of daylight vanished beyond rooftops, Sam decided that even a twenty-four-hour surveillance might not prove as productive as he would like, therefore, because after today he wouldn't have the time himself, whichever detective Lieutenant Stokes detached for the purpose of picking up Borzoi's trail would have to forego passive surveillance and make a tactful canvass to find the fugitive.

With his mind made up on that score, Sam returned to the sedan, put a call through for Lieutenant Stokes, and reported his conclusions. Stokes was perfectly agreeable, saying he would dispatch a man at once. He then asked if Sam intended to do any more today, and Sam took perverse pleasure in saying he would like to meet Stokes on the deserted old docks east of the Asche and Cohn warehouse. He also requested that Stokes contact that undercover man he had in the vicinity of the tenement district, and have him at the rendezvous too.

Lieutenant Stokes agreed, but without

much verve. 'Wouldn't early morning be just as well, Sam?'

Adams smiled. 'I think not, Lieutenant. Delay isn't going to help us, and it just might hurt us. I'll be down there in half an hour.'

After leaving the precious parking place and turning at the nearest corner to begin the long run to skid-row, Sam chuckled. The primary difference between a working detective and an administrative police officer, was social. Richard Stokes had for years left his office at five o'clock and had been under few compulsions to return to it until eight the following morning. If he ever got summonses at night he could handily delegate whatever they demanded of him, to an underling such as Sam Adams. It was soul-satisfying to Sam Adams to be driving now to a meeting that might interfere with Lieutenant Stokes's social night-life.

Of course Sam's conscience scolded him, but he could endure that without too much discomfort since the voice of conscience is invariably weak and small. Had Helen Moran been in the car with Sam it might have been different; her voice, under provocation, could be quite strident and unpleasant. But Helen, he felt confident, would be at home preparing her dinner by now, and afterwards, oblivious of Sam's whereabouts, she would either curl up with a good book, or sit and watch television.

Track, along toward day's end, was snail-paced and frustrating, but that didn't bother Sam much. He had burglary in mind and the gloaming was not conducive to successful breaking and entering. But by the time he ultimately reached the docks it had been slightly more than an hour from the time he'd spoken to Lieutenant Stokes.

There was one mitigating factor. What frustrated one person could under the circumstances be relied upon to frustrate another person. Although the undercover man was on hand when Sam parked the car and left it to go strolling through the gathering gloom, Lieutenant Stokes had not yet arrived, undoubtedly also caught up and delayed by traffic.

The undercover man looked even seedier and disreputable in the gloaming. He didn't smile as Sam approached although he nodded. Evidently the role he was portraying was infecting his outlook a little.

Sam, still feeling maliciously pleased, asked what had occurred around the tenement where the four pseudo alcoholics were holding up. The undercover man said there had been very little outside activity. He'd kept a close watch since his earlier conversation with Sam, but the suspects hadn't shown much overt activity. Sam was encouraged rather than discouraged by this scrap of information.

'They have their work,' he said, then he smiled as Stokes's unmarked sedan eased down the deserted byway and halted. As the senior officer strode towards them Sam asked if the undercover man had heard the results of the photographer's work. The detective nodded and turned to greet his superior when Lieutenant Stokes walked up, nodding his evening greeting. Stokes looked at Sam Adams as though he were viewing a unique form of life.

'One question,' he said forthrightly. 'How do we get four men out of their rooms long enough to get inside to have a look around?'

Sam said, 'They eat, don't they?' and the undercover man nodded, saying that the pseudo alcoholics were usually quite punctual about departing for that purpose, and that furthermore they did not eat at any of the local cafes, notoriously filthy, but drove uptown somewhere and did not return for an hour or more.

'In fact, Lieutenant,' reported the disreputable-looking detective, 'since I've been on this job I've noticed that they ordinarily drive off about this time of day.'

Sam, looking at Stokes, said, 'Did you bring a camera?'

Stokes patted a pocket. 'It occurred to me.' He was being ironic towards Sam, which caused Adams mild amusement. Stokes then said, 'Also, I withdrew the man watching O'Gorman's place, but

I detailed him and two others to the tenement area — just in case.' He looked over in the direction of the Asche and Cohn warehouse. 'By the way, Sam, did you turn up Mister Borzoi?'

'Not a sign of him. If the FBI report is correct about that delicatessen, Borzoi must be a very experienced wraith.'

'What do you propose?'

'Having someone canvass the area, bearing in mind that one bad move and our bird will take wing. I explained that to you.'

Stokes was unperturbed. 'I know. And I've assigned a man.' He glanced at his wrist then looked at the undercover man. 'Ed, you studied the tenement?'

'Yes, Lieutenant. We can get in without much trouble. In fact, that entire neighbourhood doesn't have a workable lock, and after you've been down there you'll know why — there's nothing worth stealing, and no one down there worth robbing.'

Stokes, jumping his attention back and forth as stray thoughts occurred, now said, 'Sam, those narcotics people were in again this afternoon. The FBI man was a little impatient. In fact, I almost brought him along.' Stoke's thin lips lifted as though he might smile. 'Then I remembered how touchy you'd become over this case.'

Sam had no difficulty picking up the innuendo. He thought of a good answer too, but he didn't use it. Not tonight. Perhaps, after they had their fugitives in custody he'd take Stokes on in a verbal sparring match.

The undercover man lit a cigarette, looked at his watch and suggested that unless the senior officer had more to say, they'd better be moving.

They took Sam's car, which was closer, with Lieutenant Stokes in the back seat. They were all armed, and as Stokes had revealed, there would be support for them in the event of unpleasantness.

The hour was right for cruising this more or less pedestrian area, for although during daylight excepting delivery vans and the like, or prowling patrol cars, no cars as a general rule used the streets, at the end of the day this did not hold true; factory and store workers who lived somewhere beyond skid-row used the avenues getting home.

It also helped that the tenement area, which lay south and west of skid-row, was a honeycomb of low-income families where the only two status symbols were automobiles and colour television. Sam's sedan, none too clean, blended perfectly, and it didn't offend any pedestrians who might have looked, having that disreputable-looking pseudo wino in the front seat beside Sam.

He guided them to a littered vacant lot on an adjacent street where they left the car, by which time it was quite dark all around, and quite still, which probably meant that most of the tenement-district inhabitants were either at the bars or at supper.

Sam thought he'd spotted the surveillance team, not far from the particular tenement their unkempt companion pointed out as the one they sought. Stokes, being unable because of distance and lowering darkness to be certain, merely shrugged.

The buildings were side by side. In

fact, the south wall of one tenement was also the north wall of its neighbour. None of the buildings were over three stories tall, and atop every one of them television aerials bristled like spiky bones of pale silver.

People strolled occasionally, or loitered near delapidated doorsteps, their colour ranging from Nordic white to Afric black, with every shade of the spectrum in between.

The air was strongly scented from greasy cooking, from strong tobacco, from car exhaust fumes and from the universal sweet-sour, somewhat oniony scent of poverty, which was by no means a figment of anyone's imagination.

The particular building Sam and his associates paused to study was lighted on the first two levels, but the top level was utterly dark. Sam asked their guide about that. The man said, 'They're out to dinner, like I thought they would be. But I wish I knew how long ago they'd left, then I'd know how much time we've got.'

Stokes nudged the undercover man.

'Lead out, Ed. Let's get this over with.'

Ed moved up the littered sidewalk in a deliberate shuffle heading for an alleyway into which he stepped, made sure the others were behind him, then he abandoned the shuffle and hastily cut into a filthy, refuse mounded back-area, walking through darkness as though he'd been here before, which he doubtless had.

He stopped where a broken rear door sagged, looked at Adams, at Stokes, then shouldered the door aside and stepped into a pitch-black and very smelly hallway that had whisperings of radio and television sounds its full length.

They were inside the building, which meant they were now irretrievably committed.

15

Cornered!

Fortunately those sounds of music and voices were adequately loud to conceal the sound of creaking floors and stairs, for otherwise every foot covered by the three policemen would have been telegraphed from one part of the old building to another part.

Fortunately too, none of the people sitting soporifically watching television's pseudo-sophisticates — whom they alternately envied and despised — cared one whoop in hell who might be going up or down the stairs beyond their doorways.

Sam, who was directly behind the undercover man, stepped past an ajar door and saw a paunchy man in his undershirt and stocking feet, sitting sprawled in an old overstuffed chair, beer can in hand, hypnotically watching his boob-tune.

A slatternly woman running to lard lay upon a broken divan and in a corner a filthy baby sucked a filthy rag, also staring at the only light in the room — that television set.

It was, Sam fleetingly thought, a representative example of probably every one in every tenement building for miles in every direction.

The undercover man halted on the first-floor landing, looked around at Lieutenant Stokes as though seeking instructions, and when Sam gave him a light shove and growled, the undercover man started up the second flight of stairs without a word.

Stokes unbuttoned his jacket on the second landing. He did it discreetly but Sam noticed. So did the other policeman, who was up front. Stokes made a little impatient gesture and they started the final climb.

On the third-floor landing there was a very strong odour of onions. The landing reeked of it. Stokes made a grimace and Sam winked at him. 'Heroin has a very unique smell. Onions don't.' He tapped their guide on the shoulder, pointing towards a door with a new hasp and padlock on it. 'What have you in mind for that?'

The undercover man smiled for the first time, reached under his shapeless old coat and brought forth a rachet screwdriver. A very common oversight, that. The screwdriver made very short work of removing four screws that just happened to be on the wrong side of the door. If the hasp had been installed on the *inside*, obviously it couldn't have been rendered useless so readily.

Stokes watched impassively. There were some avenues in which policemen were more sophisticated, or just more experienced, than some felons — excluding, of course, professional burglars.

The door was propped aside, they entered a scantily furnished parlour-of-sorts, with several unrolled sleeping bags on metal cots, and were helped through the gloom by a very obliging street-lamp not far distant, outside, which cast a kind of milky, pale glow throughout the place.

Sam moved towards the cramped kitchen and found what he'd thought would have to be in that room, since no other room in the apartment would have a stove as well as running water.

There was a huge galvanized pair of tubs taking up nearly the entire kitchen floor space. There were several buckets on the cold stove and some kind of drying device had been rigged up in front of a doorless oven, utilizing taut wires stretched in front of the oven-opening, and below that was a convex glass shelf running beyond the stove.

But there was no bolt of cloth drying, and as far as Sam could detect from the doorway, there were no bolts anywhere in the room. He verified this by edging round the floor-tubs to open and close each little cupboard. Except some filthy dishes with withered shreds of uneaten food still adhering to them, and a canister of coffee, there was very little in the cupboards. Sam was turning away when Lieutenant Stokes came to the kitchen doorway to stand a moment studying the improvised drying equipment, then to say, 'Come in the bedroom, Sam.'

The undercover detective was down on his knees before a metal box he'd taken from beneath an old broken bed upon which lay some soiled working clothes. In one corner of this room someone had plugged in a hot-plate, which sat upon the floor. A large pan holding boiled onions was on the hot-plate. This, unquestionably, was what provided the camouflaging stench they'd noticed outside on the landing.

As Sam and Stokes returned, the undercover detective grunted to his feet and held forth two bundles. One was of bank notes held securely by an elastic band, the other bundle was of crumpled brocade which had been removed from a wrinkled paper sack.

Sam ignored the money and put his tongue to the brocade. It did not have the bitter taste it should have had, meaning of course that it had already been cooked and dried to leach out the heroin. He handed it back making a motion for the detective to put it back where he'd found it.

Lieutenant Stokes was fitting a flash-bulb to his camera as Sam went probing through this room. He located one tin of heroin crystals and one un-touched bolt of silk in a small closet.

He left Stokes taking pictures, examined the bathroom, then, catching sight of a heavy car easing into the alleyway down below and to his right, he hastened back to alert his companions. He had no idea that this might be the suspects returning, but he was satisfied with all he'd seen anyway, and as he said to Stokes, there was no point in continuing to tempt fate. Stokes had used his last bulb so they left the apartment, stood impatiently waiting for the undercover man to replace the hasp, then they were on the point of starting down towards the second-floor landing when someone clumping up from below made them freeze in their tracks

Sam turned frantically. There were two other doors on this floor, both on the opposite side from the apartment they'd just burglarized. At the far end of the grimy corridor was a window. Sam whipped around heading in that direction. It was customary to have a window at the end of each hallway, and it was also customary — obligatory in fact, according to the State building and safety code — for there to be a fire-escape landing or ladder beyond the window.

Sam got to the window with Stokes and their companion close by, but the frame was weathered and warped and could not be raised.

Someone on the second floor laughed, evidently at something amusing said by another person, then there was the sound of men's heavy, cadenced steps beginning the final climb.

Lieutenant Stokes reached with both hands, the right one going out of sight beneath his unbuttoned jacket where his service revolver lay, the left hand grasping desperately for the doorknob only a yard or two from that warped and inoperable window.

The door swung outward. Stokes didn't glance in. Neither did the men with him; as one person they stepped past the door into a closet where someone had once kept buckets, brooms, rags, and which was now inhabited by terrified mice whose squealings and scratchy little frantic sounds made Lieutenant Stokes stamp at something that blindly tried to rush up his trouser leg.

Sam eased the door closed. It was tight and very, very dark in the broom-closet. It was also unpleasantly sour-smelling. Outside, a man's gravelly voice mumbled and a second masculine answered, then there was the unmistakable sound of men moving from the landing down the gloomy hall towards the padlocked door. For moments there was no additional sound, but when the door was opened it did so on dry hinges. One of the men out there spoke without much conviction, saying it wouldn't do any harm to oil the hinge that was noisy. The deep-down grumbling voice had an almost indifferent reply to offer.

'For why? We can stand it for another couple of days.'

The door was noisily closed.

For another fifteen seconds the cramped detectives remained motionless and scarcely breathing. Lieutenant Stokes eventually

190

reached, caught hold of the knob and began to very cautiously twist it to the right. This particular door did not squeak, but from the lower end of the corridor to the front area where the stairs were, there was hardly one solid board in the floor.

Sam brushed his lips with a finger as he moved gingerly out of the closet, bent and methodically removed his shoes. Stokes and the other policeman did the same, then, with Sam staying as close as he could get to the left-hand wall of the corridor, where the floorboards were at least held down by the studding and panelling, they started their breathless withdrawal.

Downstairs someone turned up a radio or a television set and momentarily there was raucous music. But that lasted only until someone else could indignantly turn down the volume. Otherwise, although sound permeated the entire building, it was less noticeable upon the third floor.

The suspects beyond that door with the new hasp and padlock must have been averse to music; not a sound came from beyond their door. What made it infinitely worse, as Sam eased past, the flooring began to protest anew over Sam's rather considerable weight.

Stokes had his revolver palmed and the undercover detective had a hand hidden beneath his coat. Sam had to flatten along the wall as a man's voice beyond the door opposite, came through clearly but not too distinctly, saying something about a malfunctioning electric device. Sam nor his companions made any attempt to divine what kind of device the man was referring to; they were only about twelve feet from the stairway now.

Down on the second floor a door slammed. Sam had reached the landing when that happened and did not pause as he began to descend. Behind him Stokes and the other detectives came on stocking-feet, as soundless as shadows.

Sam paused as though about to put his shoes back on — they would certainly appear a lot less ludicrous, if not downright suspicious, wearing their shoes, than carrying them.

But Sam changed his mind and for an excellent reason; it was quite dark on the second floor landing. The naked bulb hanging midway along the corridor had burnt out. At least it was not giving off any illumination so they got past that floor and started down towards the ground-level landing, and here, midway, Sam did stop, lean upon the wall and slip back into his shoes. He also paused to wipe perspiration from his forehead and neck, then, no longer trying to conceal their passage, the three men trooped on down. Ironically enough, after having escaped detection upon the third and second landings, down on the ground-floor where it wouldn't have mattered if they'd been seen, not a soul was in sight. They left the building the same way they'd entered it, by the broken rear door, and paused just once to exchange relieved glances before being led back into the alleyway again.

There, they encountered the car whose arrival had warned Sam the suspects were returning. Stokes paused briefly to reach inside to twist the registration certificate face-up, but it was too dark to make out a name, and while Stokes probably had a torch in a pocket he wisely did not use it. They sidled past the car and reached the street. There, Stokes turned back to note the licence plate and write it in a notebook before striding forth to catch up with Sam and the other detective.

It had been a very near thing and Sam was still a little upset. As he told the others, while crossing the street heading over where they'd left his sedan, there wouldn't have been a way in the world to mitigate anything back there, if they'd been caught.

It was, of course, a fact, but it was just as much a fact that they *hadn't* been caught back there.

As they were driving back in the general direction of the abandoned old docks the undercover detective said Sam could drop him off anywhere close by, that he had to meet his relief-man not far from O'Gorman's tavern.

Sam and Lieutenant Stokes arrived back where Stokes had left his car without the other detective. Sam lit a cigarette, blew out a grey cloud and said, 'We can proceed on the evidence of that cloth in the flat.'

'And my photographs,' added Stokes. 'When — in the morning?'

Sam shook his head. 'Not quite. I want Borzoi. Those four punks in the tenement are all locals; we can hunt them down any time. But if Borzoi gets the wind up my guess is that he'll get out of the country.'

Stokes opened the door, climbed out of Sam's car, turned and bent down as he said, 'Handle it your way, Sam. I'll be in early in case you want me for anything. Good night.'

Sam nodded, watched Stokes go to his own car, turn and head back uptown. He didn't do that, himself, until he'd finished the cigarette, but eventually he did. By then it was almost ten o'clock, which meant Sam Adams was not going to get to bed early this night either.

16

An Interloper

There were two minor crises the following morning, and the first one bothered Sam much more than the second one.

That detective Lieutenant Stokes had sent into the neighbourhood of the delicatessen had come up with absolutely nothing. No one he'd struck up a conversation with mentioned a flashy-dresser in the neighbourhood, who owned a black car.

Sam went along to Stokes's office to talk personally to the detective, but that elicited nothing further. Stokes detailed another man to the area to continue the search.

That was what bothered Sam. The second crisis was less critical although it had slightly more unpleasant overtones. The FBI man, who had incorporated the interest of the national narcotics agency's man with his own professional interest, because the other agent had been summoned back to Washington the night before, was critical of Sam's efforts.

It wasn't a matter of great concern to Sam that this was so. As he told the FBI man, *his* case was still primarily a matter of murder.

The agent scoffed. 'One wino, Mister Adams. They go down the drain every day. Borzoi is a big catch. Our information makes it mandatory that he be apprehended before he can sneak away again. There is an international connection here.'

Sam agreed amiably. 'We'll get him, if he's still in the country.'

That did not seem to reassure the FBI agent. 'What I'd like to do is bring in a couple more of our men and take over that end of the case from you.'

Sam remained amiable for a very good reason: without wholehearted local permission and approval, the Federal Bureau of Investigation could not interfere. As a general rule the FBI was invited to participate. Otherwise, as anxious as it might be to become involved, local authorities did not have to grant permission.

'We'll find him,' reiterated Sam, as Helen appeared in the doorway of his private office to say Lieutenant Stokes was on the line.

Sam punched the intercom button, picked up the telephone and leaned back in his chair. 'Lieutenant . . . ?'

'The stake-out down at O'Gorman's place just called in, Sam. The tavern was hit last night.'

'Hit? How?'

'Burglary. Ransacked.'

Sam's brows briefly knit, then his expression cleared. 'Howard Wax didn't believe it when O'Gorman told him Franz Ludwig did not have O'Gorman keep things for him. Was anything stolen?'

'A few bottles of cheap wine. My guess is that this was only done to make it appear winos were the burglars. Otherwise, the door-lock was picked without any forcing. Winos wouldn't do that.'

Sam nodded. 'Probably our friends from the tenement. Wax might have done it, but there is no forcible entry on his rap-sheet. Okay, Lieutenant, thanks. By the way, has the lad from the delicatessen-surveillance called anything in?'

'Not a word. Sam? Is that FBI man with you?'

'Yeah.'

'I understand he wants to bring in some of their men and take over the Borzoi end of things.'

'Yeah.'

'What do you think?'

'Not under any circumstances, Lieutenant, and you can tell that to Chief Hall.'

Stokes said, 'I understand. I'll take care of it.'

As Sam replaced the telephone he smiled at the visitor sitting beside his desk. 'They sure don't give up easy. If they knew where that bolt of impregnated brocade was they'd scatter like quail. They burglarized a skid-row dive last night searching for the cloth.'

The agent said, 'I just came up from the laboratory. They've worked out a system for re-claiming the heroin. It's very ingenious.'

'So was the system of getting the stuff soaked into that cloth.'

The agent nodded, studied Sam a moment then said, 'To get back where we were . . . '

'Just be a little patient,' exclaimed Sam.

'Suppose I go upstairs, Mister Adams?'

Sam stopped looking so amiable as he rose, stepped around the desk and walked heavily to the door, which he opened. 'Be my guest.'

The agent rose, studied Sam a moment, then as he crossed towards the door he said, 'That was the part of the telephone call I couldn't pick up, wasn't it?'

Sam nodded candidly, let the other man walk past, then smiled and closed the door leaving the FBI man in the outer office with Helen. He didn't remain there any longer than it took him to glare venomously at Sam's closed door, then stalk out of the office.

Helen came to rap on the door and Sam opened it at once, looked past making certain his caller had indeed departed, then left the door wide and went back around behind the desk as he said, 'We're boxed-in, Curly-head. We've got everything we need to move in and bust the whole crew — except the key man.'

'Robert Borzoi,' she said, coming closer to the desk. 'Sam, another teletype message just came in from the Hong Kong authorities.'

'What did it say?'

'That your story of heroin-saturated cloth had been verified at their end and they were going to make a careful investigation before making any arrests, in order to be sure of nabbing everyone connected with the ring at their end.'

Sam said, 'Decent of them. It could queer the works at our end if they ran out and grabbed the first few suspects. Borzoi would get the word at once, then we really would lose him.'

'Sam, why don't you let the FBI help with Mister Borzoi?'

'For the same reason I don't want Dick Stokes sticking his big blundering beak in. I've got things pretty well coming our way. Everything is very critical right now.

Just one blunder by some well-intentioned federal man and everyone disappears into thin air.' He lit a cigarette, eyeing her. 'I'm holding my breath, that's how close we are to making a fool-proof case. Just the whereabouts of one man is keeping us from moving. We should know where that one is by nightfall.'

'And if you don't know, Sam?'

'Look, Curly-head, as long as Howard Wax, Borzoi, and those four punks at the tenement have no idea the police are practically breathing down their necks, no one is going to blow the whistle. We can afford another day, maybe. But right now we're balancing on the razor's edge. Do you understand? The more people getting involved the more danger of a blunder.'

Helen nodded, and whether she agreed or not, did not press the issue. Normally, with a routine case and an uninterrupted environmental pattern, Sam Adams was a big, somewhat phlegmatic individual. But he'd missed a good deal of sleep lately, and had cracked a very difficult case which was hanging now by a thread; he would not continue to be pleasant if anyone, including Helen, raveled his nerves.

She was proved correct sometime later when Chief Hall descended from Olympus to the lysol-scented second-floor to inform Sam that the FBI man had telephoned his chief in Washington, to have his chief call Hall with a formal request that the FBI be permitted to participate in the pursuit and apprehension of Robert Borzoi.

Sam's face got pale but otherwise his expression remained gentle. He said, 'Chief, I have all the respect in the world for the Bureau, but I also know from experience that when new people move in at a critical point, even in a case a lot less important than this one is, you are definitely increasing your chances for failure.'

Hall thought that over then said, 'Dick Stokes' view-point too. All right, Sam.' He left the office without another word, but it was safe to assume he would return the Bureau's call, denying permission for FBI intervention.

Helen appeared in the doorway. 'It

is lunchtime, Sam. You will ruin your constitution eating and sleeping the way you do. Put your coat on and come along.'

He smashed out the cigarette he'd been smoking, stared a moment then rose. 'I hope Borzoi takes time out to eat,' he said, as he joined her at the door. 'There,' he said, 'I thought you and Margery Fein would be having lunch together.'

She looked surprised. 'Why?'

'Well, didn't you tell me recently that she'd just got married?'

Helen rolled her eyes heavenward. 'Sam, for heaven's sake, all I said was that she and a man named — '

'I remember the name. Garfunckel. Who could ever forget that?'

'Are you going to wear your hat, Sam? It's been hanging on that rack for a month.'

He looked at the hat and walked past it. 'With any luck, maybe someone will steal it. I loathe hats.'

They descended to the ground-floor and discovered that taking the midday

204

break precisely on time was not very wise. People were pouring out of the lifts, out of offices and corridors on all sides. By the time they got through the front doors to the sidewalk they'd been hailed and greeted and bumped into by almost everyone either of them knew in the building, including one 'girl' of forty-five who had flaming red hair and startlingly blue-shadowed eyes who gave Sam a playful gouge in the ribs as she said,

'Why don't you up and marry her, Mister Adams, it'd be a lot cheaper if she put up a pack lunch for two and stayed in the office with you at lunch-break.'

Sam smiled horribly and hastened along with Helen's arm locked inside his arm next to the ribs. Out of earshot he said, 'If there's one frightening thing about Civil Service it's that the system perpetuates the genuine worthless people of this earth, and someday I predict they'll outnumber the others. Then where'll we be?'

Helen said, 'Going to lunch just like everyone else, I suppose.'

They got a table at a restaurant, ordered spaghetti, which she told him was very starchy and difficult to digest, along with being ruinously fattening, and he told her that he liked spaghetti, had been eating it all his mature years, and proposed to go right on eating it, since he had no reason to believe he was going to live forever anyway, and had never possessed the kind of physique that ad-men sought.

She cocked her head at him as though believing he was on the verge of a foul mood, then said, 'Tell me what's gone *right* the last day or two, Sam.'

That was a good ploy. Perhaps he recognized it as such too, but in any case he leaned across the table and recounted the adventure of the night before when he and Stokes and that other detective had performed a genuine act of burglary.

She smiled when he detailed how they'd barely managed to escape undetected. Then she said, 'I forgot to tell you, but there's been so much traffic through the office this morning.'

'Tell me what?'

'Margery confided in me that Lieutenant Stokes put your name in for promotion to sergeant of detectives.'

Sam was shocked. 'When?'

She smiled again. 'Yesterday, right after you and he had that terrible argument, and he went back to his office as red as a beet.'

Sam thought that over for a while, and their meals arrived — two thick dishes heaped with greasy, reddish-tinted spaghetti.

Afterwards he ate, found that he had been ravenously hungry without being aware of it, and scarcely said another word until all the pleats had been smoothed out of his stomach. Then he lit a cigarette, sipped black coffee and watched Helen pick at a salad she'd turned to after eating only a few mouthfuls of the spaghetti.

'If it's approved,' he said, 'it'll mean quite a bit more salary.'

'And more responsibility, Sam. You won't have to go out on cases at night any more.'

He inhaled, exhaled, glanced around

the noisy, crowded room, glanced back and said, 'I don't need more money. I'm getting by all right.'

She put down her fork. 'Sam Adams, do you want to always be just another plodding detective? Don't you aspire to something better — something more fulfilling?'

'Like what?'

She blushed furiously, ducked her head and went back to stabbing the lettuce and tomato in her salad.

17

Lost and Found

Lieutenant Stokes came to Sam's office the next morning to disconsolately report that the second detective he'd assigned to the delicatessen store had also returned with no word of anyone answering Robert Borzoi's description. That same detective had suggested to Stokes that just possibly the FBI report giving the store as Borzoi's last known address may never have been correct, or else it may have been correct at one time, and now no longer was.

Sam was tempted to seek out that FBI agent who'd annoyed him the day before, but in the end he suggested that he and Stokes go back to the delicatessen. Stokes was agreeable.

They decided, after parking the car in an area posted for the exclusive use of lorries, that Lieutenant Stokes should go boldly along to the delicatessen and during the course of making purchases, see if he couldn't pick up some information.

Sam would wait in the Department sedan, which he did, and as he waited, Sam also read the morning paper.

It was a pleasant morning. Every now and then Sam was able to catch sight of the sky. There was probably a high wind blowing to cause those rents in the layers of smoggy overcast that perpetually shrouded the countryside.

It was warm without being hot, although undoubtedly later on in the day there would be plenty of heat. Spring in the city was just as much a blessing as it was elsewhere, with the exception that city-people had to carry it around in their hearts and imaginations, for in the city few trees budded without blight, and fewer flowers responded to the promise of renewed life.

The heat more than anything told city-dwellers that spring was waning and summer was taking its place. As far as Sam Adams was concerned, summer was long overdue. Sam was one of those oily-skinned individuals who neither suffered nor sunburned. He enjoyed heat and did *not* enjoy cold.

But sitting somnolently in a warm car reading a soporific newspaper also helped the increasing heat; Sam almost dozed off. He undoubtedly would have except that Lieutenant Stokes returned with some pastrami, some braunschweiger and some chopped chicken liver, which he magnanimously offered to Sam on the basis that Sam being a bachelor, could use pre-cooked food.

Sam put aside his newspaper, tossed the packages Stokes dropped in his lap over on to the back seat, and showed a little impatience as he asked what the lieutenant had learned.

'Nothing our two detectives couldn't have learned if you hadn't put the delicatessen itself off-limits. There was a man answering Borzoi's description who had a room rented upstairs over the delicatessen, but a few days ago he checked out.'

Sam said, 'I'm afraid to ask . . . '

'They had no idea where he moved to.'

Sam nodded. 'That's what I meant.' He started the car. 'Maybe he moved into a BOAC pressurized cabin bound for Hong Kong.'

'Don't you want to go look at the room he had?' Stokes asked as they began working out into mid-morning traffic.

'You can send someone else to do that, Lieutenant. I want to locate Mister Borzoi.'

Back at the building they parted, Stokes heading for his office, Sam Adams stopping by a cigarette-vending machine to purchase a mentholated packet, then going on to his office.

Helen was sympathetic, which ordinarily evokes appreciation, sometimes maudlin appreciation, in chastened men. Instead, Sam Adams told her to telephone the records division of the four major borough-wide banking institutions, make certain they understood this was official police business, then inquire whether anyone answering to the names of the aliases attributed to Robert Borzoi, had an account, and if so, at which branch office.

While she was doing that, Sam went to his private office to make a similar enquiry of the Bureau of Certificates, New York State Department of Automobile Registration.

Finally, he telephoned an acquaintance at the Port Authority, Immigration Division, and here he learned that although Robert Borzoi had actually been naturalized, becoming a US citizen some eleven years previously, he still chose to refer to himself as a British subject, a resident of Hong Kong.

Sam's reaction to this was cynical. 'Yeah. And the moment he debarks in Hong Kong or London, he runs up the Stars and Stripes. I know the type. Whichever country they happen to be in is told they belong to some other country. I don't know what that's supposed to prove, or prevent, but if I can get my hands on that bird this time I think I can settle the question of his residency for the next few years. But first I've got to find him.'

The Port Authority had an address. In fact, it had several, and each was even more useless than the recent address Sam had been supplied by the FBI.

Just before going out to lunch Sam stopped down in Communications to send off a wireless message to the Hong Kong authorities requesting anything they had on where Borzoi might be found while in New York.

He'd barely returned from lunch when Lieutenant Stokes sauntered in to say the narcotics people had reported a considerable increase in sales and arrests throughout Harlem.

'Hard drugs,' reported Stokes. 'Heroin. Sam, we have one bolt of that cloth. How many other bolts were there?'

Sam grimaced. 'I'm afraid to tell you, Lieutenant. Forty-five.'

Stokes gave a little start. 'Hell Sam, there was only one left in the tenement. Did those men process all the other bolts? It doesn't seem possible.'

It was possible all right, Sam explained. He'd been sure they'd just about finished their processing when he'd heard one of those men say something about not bothering with a squeaky door because they'd only be around another couple of days.

Stokes said, 'I hate to say it, Sam, but we can't wait any longer. Even if this Borzoi-character gets clear, that's better than running the risk of losing the entire band.'

Helen called. The car-registration bureaux was on the line. He asked her to jot down the message, put down the telephone and said, 'Lieutenant, letting Borzoi get away won't just bring the FBI down on you, it'll also practically guarantee that this new system for smuggling heroin into the country will spread from coast to coast, and before someone comes up with a simple detection process, the US will be flooded with Red Chinese narcotics.'

'Listen, Sam — '

'*You* listen: If we have to make that kind of choice, which I don't see us having to make, I'd say let everyone else go and concentrate on Borzoi.'

'What kind of sense is that, Sam? Borzoi is one man, an alien. He'll leave the country.'

'What's the difference whether he peddles his junk here or in London, Berlin, Athens, or Rio de Janeiro, he's infecting people with a kind of misery no one should be allowed to spread around. Lieutenant, if you could stop the Borzois in this world, the punks that are in that old tenement getting ready to move on where they'll pick up the next forty-five bolts of impregnated cloth to wring out, couldn't get any narcotics. I say Borzoi is *the* one.'

Lieutenant Stokes rose. 'I'll get back to you,' he said, and walked out of the office. He'd barely cleared the front door when Helen came to hand Sam a slip of paper upon which she'd transcribed an address.

'From the auto registration people,' she explained. 'He's got the black sedan listed under his proper name. He'd just about have to, since comparisons are made of thumb-prints of registered car owners and people with drunk-driving records, or with suspended operator permits, not to mention local felony police files.'

Sam smiled. 'You're a wizard, Curly-head.' He rose and reached for the coat he'd shed earlier. 'I'll go and run this new address down.'

She looked up. 'With Lieutenant Stokes?'

'No, Curly-head, and it'd be just fine with me if he didn't know where I've gone. I have a sneaking suspicion that he's gone upstairs to ask Chief Hall to either take me off the case, or make me let Stokes run things.'

Sam stepped over close, winked, then moved on past Helen into the outer office and beyond, into the lysol-scented corridor where he used the stairs to reach ground level.

The fresh address for Borzoi was several miles distant, which was practically the same thing in any large city as moving into an entirely new community, which in a sense was what it amounted to.

The neighbourhood was in no way to be compared with skid-row, where Sam was convinced Borzoi had shot Franz Ludwig to death. There were cleaner stores, more ornate apartment

217

houses, even trees along the boulevard and side-streets.

Sam located the address the car-registry people had given Helen, cruised round the neighbourhood for a bit getting to know the streets, stores, residential squares, then he took up position on a side-street for a period of quiet surveillance of the dignified brownstone building where Robert Borzoi allegedly lived now.

It was different, in this area, trying to be unobtrusive. There was very little traffic, car or pedestrian, so a parked vehicle, particularly with a man sitting in it, was unusual enough to arouse mild interest.

Sam left the car a half mile away, along a boulevard where mainstream traffic and commercial storefronts stood side by side, and walked back to keep an eye on Borzoi's brownstone.

He didn't contact Helen before leaving the car, which he should have done of course; police departments the world over want to know where every on-duty man is at any given time. Detectives had some leeway in this regard, but not quite as much as Sam took. He intended to return shortly, which at least lifted his neglect from the realm of deliberate dereliction.

But as things turned out, it took quite a while to walk both ways, to and from the car, and it also used up some more time, standing prudently distant making certain Borzoi was not at the new address. By the time he got back to the car the sun was turning slightly red and inching its way down the westerly sky.

He called in, got Helen, and she told him in a flat and unemotional voice that Chief Hall wanted Sam to come upstairs the moment he returned to the office.

Sam said, 'Bad?'

'Did you ever hear of him calling someone up there, Sam, because it was *good?* I think your promotion has gone down the drain.'

'Why should you sound so disconsolate, *I'm* the one who's losing out.'

'Because two really cannot live as cheaply as one, that's why I'm disconsolate. When are you coming in?'

'Half an hour.'

'Is *he* at the new address?'

'No sign of him, no sign of the black car. I'll make a final run past on my way in. What else?'

'Lieutenant Stokes pops his head in the door every few minutes.'

'Okay, I'll see you in a while.'

Sam was as good as his word; after replacing the transceiver mouthpiece on its dashboard hook, he drove around several rows of houses and went cruising up past the brownstone house, and this time there was a sleek black car parked out front whose licence numbers tallied perfectly with the numbers Sam knew belonged to Robert Borzoi's vehicle. He drove another two squares before considering the idea of going back there, bursting in and making the arrest.

He didn't, and before too many hours had passed he was going to lament the passing of this splendid opportunity. The reason he didn't go back was that he'd told Helen he'd return to the office, and because he did not want to keep Chief Hall waiting past quitting time.

Police chiefs were just like all other

administrative officers, they did not like working overtime, particularly when there was no such thing as overtime pay.

He reached the building about four o'clock, ran upstairs to his own office, stepped in and when Helen jerked her thumb upwards, he ducked back out and rode the lift to the top floor where Chief Hall's receptionist looked at him as though he were indeed a very unique specimen of otherworld life, then she punched a button, announced him, and pointed grimly towards the closed door with the Chief's name and rank emblazoned upon it in nothing less than raised, golden lettering.

18

A Fresh Beginning

Lieutenant Stokes was in the room too, which did not surprise Sam very much, and Chief Hall, forbiddingly puffing on a pipe, looked Sam over with iceberg eyes as he gestured for Sam to take the vacant chair in front of the desk.

Reddening sunlight slanted through a louvred window and a silent air-conditioner made the office quite cool and comfortable. It also did a fair job of disposing of the pipe-smoke.

'We've been trying to locate you,' said Hall, in his chilliest tone of voice.

'I was on a stake-out,' said Sam, putting a cool, reproachful glance upon Richard Stokes.

Hall, a man who measured all things by degrees of success or failure, said, 'Is that so; what stake-out?'

'Borzoi's residence.'

Lieutenant Stokes looked up swiftly, but he still kept silent. Chief Hall removed his pipe, laid it tenderly in an ashtray and leaned with both elbows on his large desk. 'Borzoi's residence,' he repeated quietly. 'And was he at this one, Mister Adams?'

'Not when I first ran it down and staked it out, but as I was leaving the area his car was parked out front. I think he's there.'

Chief Hall said, 'That's convenient, because you see we've lost the other four men.'

Sam was jolted. 'From the tenement?'

Chief Hall nodded and handed Stokes the initiative by simply raising his eyebrows in Stokes's direction. The lieutenant met Sam's enquiring glance levelly.

'After we talked in your office, Sam, I had the undercover detective down by the tenement make certain we could corral that bunch before I took a flying-squad and jumped them. He hadn't seen them leave the apartment all morning and assumed they were still there. The car

223

we saw last night was parked in the alley.'

Sam sighed and went rummaging through coat pockets for the packet of mentholated cigarettes, found it, extract-one and lit up. Stokes spoke on.

'They'd abandoned that car, the apartment was cleaned out, the men gone.'

For five seconds the office was totally quiet. Chief Hall reached to pick up his pipe, finally, but before he could speak Sam beat him to it.

'*Maybe* they discovered we'd burglarized their flat, but my guess is that they did not.'

Hall was sardonic. 'No? Then why did they flee?'

'They didn't flee, Chief, they were finished. They'd wrung-out the bolts of cloth, had handed over all the re-claimed heroin except for one bolt, and we actually heard one of them mention pulling out within the next couple of days anyway.'

'So . . . ?'

'Borzoi got a new address in a fresh

neighbourhood. My guess is that there is another shipment of cloth on the way to some new outlet in the new district. Borzoi went ahead to set everything up. As soon as the new shipment arrives, they'll get their hands on it — probably exactly as they did before, by burglarizing some warehouse, some store possibly — then they'll be back in the re-claiming business.'

Chief Hall neglected to light his pipe, put it down again and frowned at Lieutenant Stokes. 'Dick, any comments?'

Stokes shook his head. 'I only hope he's right, sir.'

Hall said, 'Yeah. He'd better be. All right, you two check this out. And *this* time make some arrests. Go on now.'

Stokes led the way out of Chief Hall's office into the yonder lighted corridor. In front of the lift he turned and said, 'Sam, I'm not much of a praying man, but this minute I could start becoming one.'

Adams was a little cool when he replied. 'Thanks for turning me in to the Chief. As for the prayers, save them. At least until we find out if Howard

Wax quit Asche and Cohn. And if he did quit them, then pray we can find the new outfit he's gone to work for, because that's where the shipment of silk and brocade will turn up.'

They rode down to the second floor where Stokes accompanied Sam into the little office he shared with Helen. She should have been gone, it was now past five o'clock. Instead she was standing behind her desk looking pale and tense. The moment Sam and Stokes entered she held forth a teletype message for Sam.

'The Hong Kong answer to your request for Borzoi's stateside contacts and addresses. Sam, it says the British police have dug up an address, but it's not Borzoi's, it's the address of a New York City interior decorating company that has been consigned a shipment of twenty-five bolts of brocade and silk from the same company that consigned the same kind of cloth to Asche and Cohn!'

Lieutenant Stokes sprang over to read the message Sam was holding in both hands. Stokes said, somewhat fervently, 'Thank God.'

'And Her Majesty's overseas authorities,' put in Sam, pocketing the piece of paper and glancing at his watch. 'If you'd care to ride along, Lieutenant, I think we'd better go and see Mister Asche or Mister Cohn to verify that their man Wax is no longer employed at the warehouse, then we'd better go and hunt up this interior decorating outfit and do a little snooping.'

Stokes also consulted his wristwatch, his face getting longer and longer. Sam winked at Helen, his spirits revived, but her contemplation of Lieutenant Stokes did not alter, she showed disappointment in him, and something that might have been suppressed hostility as well.

'Very well,' Stokes said eventually. 'Let's go.'

Sam hesitated, gazing at Helen. 'Dinner tomorrow night,' he said, and smiled as he turned to trail Stokes out of the office.

They stopped by the lieutenant's office very briefly, for his hat, then hiked on down to mingle with the exciting crowd of employees, none of whom seemed to have made it through the day without losing a good deal of the exuberance they may have come through those same streetside doors with, eight or more hours earlier.

They took Sam's car, not for any special reason except that Sam, striding slightly in the lead, headed in that direction.

On the drive to skid-row Sam asked if Stokes had called in the undercover men. Stokes had; in fact, he said, up until he'd seen that message from Hong Kong, he'd considered taking his vacation now instead of later in the summer. He also said that Chief Hall had called him on the Ludwig-Borzoi matter, he had not gone upstairs voluntarily.

He did not, however, mention having put Sam's name in for promotion, but then it was probably that he wouldn't have mentioned that anyway, since it did nothing to heighten morale for a detective to know he was being considered — only to have the suggestion denied.

Sam didn't really worry very much. He had never been interested in money, only in the amounts of it necessary to live decently, and now, nearly thirty-eight years of age, he was past the time in life when financial drive was likely to manifest itself.

By the time they reached the Asche and Cohn warehouse shadows were forming. Not especially dark nor long shadows, because daylight no longer departed as soon as it had a month or two before, but still, the lights had been turned on as they braked to a halt out front of the building, and inside they saw a man and a woman standing by the little desk the woman used, discussing some papers she was showing to the man.

Sam, in the act of alighting, said, 'Cohn and the secretary. We're in luck.'

As the two large men entered from the front dock two faces lifted, neither registering much delight at this late-day visit. Cohn recognized Sam Adams at once, it showed the way he blinked and seemed to turn wary.

The woman retired behind her little desk with the papers, put them aside and went into a tiny closet for her coat and hat. She was pointedly separating herself from whatever was about to ensue.

Mister Cohn shook Lieutenant Stokes's hand when Sam made the introduction, then raised inquiring eyes. 'The insurance company already paid off on that shipment of cloth,' he said, as though this should convey to both detectives that he'd washed his hands of the affair.

Sam said, 'Has Mister Wax gone home for the day?'

Cohn blinked. The woman, shrugging into her coat, shot Sam a guarded look, then started for the door. No one interfered. After she'd gone Cohn said that Howard Wax had terminated his employment the day before.

Cohn shrugged. 'No reason, except that he didn't like working down here. And I got to admit it's a lousy neighbourhood, what with those crummy winos lying in the alleyways and leaving their bottles on the loading docks every night. I should think the police ought to be able to do something about that.'

Sam looked sympathetic but when he spoke it wasn't about deplorable neighbourhood conditions at all. 'Did Mister Wax say where he was going — whether he had another job lined up or not?'

'No,' answered Cohn. 'He just said he was quitting. They don't have to give a reason any more. When I was first starting out, by gawd, when you quit a company you had to have a good reason; people were more responsible in those days.'

'Yes indeed,' said Sam. 'Did Mister Wax have any personal callers here at the warehouse, Mister Cohn?'

'Personal callers? Say, are you after Howard for something?'

'We're interested in him,' put in Stokes smoothly. 'Interested in the people he might have associated with.'

Cohn's little eyes brightened. 'Sure you are. You got some idea Howard was mixed up in the burglary, eh?'

'Has that possibility also occurred to you?' asked Sam, turning Cohn's question back.

For a moment the shorter, older man looked into their faces, then dropped his eyes and considered the floor, scuffed and lustreless, underfoot. 'Yes, the idea occurred,' he admitted. 'Why shouldn't it? Here we get a new man, and right away we're hit.'

'How about personal acquaintances, Mister Cohn?'

'I'm not around a lot of the time. Mister Asche is gone even more of the time. I only saw Howard talk to one person apart from drivers and loaders, but there may have been others.'

'This one person . . . ?'

'Drove up across the street one day right after Howard went to work for us. Youngish man; he was too far away for me to get a real good look, and I wasn't very interested at the time either. It just crossed my mind that if it happened too often during working hours I'd have to speak to Howard about it. After all, we're running a business here.'

'Late-model black car, Mister Cohn?'

'Yes. Looked new.'

'And the younger man — well-dressed, dark hair, slim, affluent-looking?'

'That's him, Mister Adams. That's him

to a T.' Cohn paused a moment. '*Was* Howard mixed up in the burglary?'

Lieutenant Stokes answered. 'It's possible. We'd like to talk to him, but we'd appreciate it even more if he comes back, or if you happen to meet him again, if you did *not* say that we were asking about him.'

Cohn said, 'Sure not,' with a heartfelt sigh. 'What's it all coming to, I'd like to know? You hire decent-looking people, pay 'em a decent wage, and what do they do? Rob you. I had a friend in the business a few years ago who had to fire a louse, and what does this louse do — sets fire to my friend's store. And what happens? Nothing. The police said they couldn't come up with sufficient evidence to bring the man to trial. How do you like that?'

Lieutenant Stokes commiserated in his most soothing manner, and as soon thereafter as he and Sam could escape, they did so.

It was beginning to turn genuinely gloomy by the time they drove out of the skid-row neighbourhood bound for that cleaner, more self-respecting area where Borzoi had rented his new set of rooms.

In fact, by the time they cruised past the brownstone where Sam pointed out the sleek, black car still parked at the kerbing where Sam had seen it several hours before, dusk was well on its way.

They had the address of the interior decorator's store, and located it without much trouble. The place looked very affluent, very large and successful and well-stocked. Of course it was closed and locked and although the night-lights glowed throughout the place, there wasn't a soul inside.

Locating the residential address of the proprietor, a man named Hale Ward, was simplified when they got Ward's name from the proprietor of a liquor store across the street, then looked up Ward's address in the telephone book.

Hale Ward lived in a very expensive high-rise apartment building. Sam and Lieutenant Stokes had originally intended to pay Ward a personal call, but as they sat in the car gazing up at that elegant apartment-house, Sam said dryly, 'Maybe we'd better go back to the office and look up Mister Ward. 'Be a hell of a blunder to tip our hand to a man who is working with the narcotics syndicate.'

19

Hale Ward

It wasn't until the following morning that they had all the information back on Hale Ward, the very successful interior decorator, and some of this information had to be gleaned from a source that never ceased denying that it gave out personal information: the Internal Revenue Service.

Actually, the IRS was solicited, not by Sam Adams or even Chief Hall. It was approached by the federal narcotics people, through whom Sam and Lieutenant Stokes worked to get the information on Ward.

Still, what they came up with, while interesting, was not very enlightening; if Hale Ward had underworld contacts no one knew it.

Ward's income was astonishing, and when one considered that he'd only been an interior decorator for six years, and prior to that time had been a US Marine, a crane-operator on construction sites, and before that a not-too-successful professional boxer, it was even more astonishing.

As Stokes said, he'd always assumed that interior decorators were very sensitive, rather aesthetic people for whom colours, combinations of colours, blends of cloth and furniture had some deeply soulful significance.

'A Marine? A boxer? A crane-operator?'

Sam laughed. 'Look at the income he had to pay tax on. He's got *something*.'

'Narcotics, Sam?'

'I don't think so, Lieutenant. The IRS runs everything through computers; maybe Hale Ward could illegally collect that money, then attribute it to his interior decorating business, but there is one flaw: every deduction, every expense, every financial outlay and intake is checked by the computer against the accounts it was supposedly paid to or derived from. *That* kind of double-checking can't be faked.' Sam lit a cigarette and leaned far back in his chair. 'Lieutenant, a man with the kind of income Mister Ward has, is not very likely to jeopardize it to pick up a few additional thousands dealing in illegal narcotics.'

Stokes was satisfied.

They left the building to drive over to the interior decorating store. It was about ten o'clock when they arrived out front, and within fifteen minutes they had learned part of the secret of a successful interior decorator.

Mister Ward, said the very beautiful and sophisticated girl who met them in the pastel office, was not in. He probably would not be in until about three o'clock in the afternoon. It was, she implied with her cool look, very presumptuous on the part of anyone, to expect Mister Hale Ward to be available to people who simply walked into the store expecting to find him there.

Properly chastened, Stokes and Sam Adams retreated to a nearby cafe for an early lunch, and to exchange a wry smile.

'The secret of success,' intoned Sam,

'is to get up before the birds and work in a trot all day long, then to go to bed devising new ways for trapping the unwary. I'd say we now know what kind of a man Mister Hale Ward is, and perhaps that explains part of his success.'

'It's the other part I'm anxious about,' said Lieutenant Stokes.

They had all the time in the world for what they did next; in fact, it was the surveillance they undertook of Hale Ward's shop that inspired them to eat an early lunch.

It paid off. From a vantage point near a taxi-stand they saw the slight, diffident-appearing man come out of Ward's shop and start down the sidewalk in the direction of a small neighbourhood cafe tucked between two much larger business establishments.

Sam said quietly, 'Howard Wax.'

Stokes's comment as they watched the former Asche and Cohn clerk shuffle along, was less direct. 'How do they do it?' He looked a little sceptical as Sam started explaining.

Sam said, 'The only real risk is Howard Wax, and I suppose he's an accomplished inside-man — clerk, book-keeper, warehouseman, file-and-correspondence — so that as soon as Borzoi gets the word concerning someone ordering the brocade and silk, Howard is sent round to get a job.'

'But he can't always be successful, Sam.'

'But it simplifies the hell out of things if he *is* successful, Lieutenant. Look how neatly it went off down at the Asche and Cohn place. And now here, with the Hale Ward outfit. Who knows how long they've been doing this or how many dozens of times Wax has been successful. And the places where he hasn't been successful, they simply go in cold and commit burglary. That's their biggest risk. With Wax on the inside to study everything, set up the robbery routine, it should be a beautiful set-up.'

They had satisfied themselves about Howard Wax, so they made a discreet study of the brownstone, and discovered something interesting over there too.

Borzoi's sleek car was still where it had been parked the late afternoon before.

'Maybe they're breaking up,' suggested Stokes.

'Borzoi's pattern seems to indicate that he's always on the move, always picking up, collecting, making contacts. If that car's been there as long as you say, Sam, I'm afraid to mention what it's beginning to look like.'

Sam was unperturbed. 'The trouble with you, Lieutenant, is that you're not a soul-brother. You don't keep the faith.'

Stokes looked around reprovingly but said nothing.

Sam smiled. 'Look, those four suspects from the tenement — they abandoned that car down there didn't they? Either because it was a stolen vehicle, or because they wanted to let people continue to think they were in the building after they'd gone, or perhaps the car was simply defective. But the point is, Lieutenant, they left the car.'

'That's no revelation,' growled Stokes.

'No,' Sam agreed, 'but it *is* a revelation how they took away their sleeping-bags and cots, their tubs and personal things. Not to mention that concave glass trough for collecting heroin particles that drop from drying cloth.'

Stokes turned and slowly gazed at Sam.

'That black car over there, Lieutenant, is how those gentlemen got out of that tenement so neatly. Perhaps parked on a back-street where your eagle-eyed surveillance chap didn't have an inkling.'

Stokes was impressed. 'Anything else?'

'Yeah. One other thing. The black car hasn't been moved since it came to rest over against the kerbing late yesterday afternoon. Wouldn't you think, since Borzoi had to take his re-claiming crew to its new location, get it set up, furnished with food, the car would have been used now, of *all* times?'

'I would think so, Sam, yes.'

'Except for one thing, Lieutenant. Borzoi's boys aren't in another tenement. They aren't creeping out at night for dinner in a decent part of town. They are right over there in that same brownstone, either in a separate apartment, in the attic, the cellar, or perhaps in the garage out back, happy as clams and setting up their re-claiming gear right this minute, more than likely.'

Lieutenant Stokes took this in stride, at least out-wardly; he glanced at his wrist and said it was time for Hale Ward to be back in his office at the interior decorating shop. Then he dropped back against the carseat and gazed thoughtfully at Borzoi's brownstone for a moment before opening his mouth again.

'You're pretty good, Sam. You've been calling some very good shots lately. But have you any idea what's going to happen if you miss this time?'

Sam shrugged thick shoulders, dropped a hard look at his superior and gave a curt answer. 'Fire me.'

He then started the car and drove quietly back towards the main boulevard.

Lieutenant Stokes said no more. They parked in the blacktopped, reserved area beside the interior decorating establishment, and although Sam said it might be better if he did not go in again, that perhaps

Wax would remember and recognize him, Stokes was willing to take the risk and said he wanted Sam with him when they braced Hale Ward.

As things turned out Stokes's idea was valid. Hale Ward was in his private office, coat and tie off, air-conditioner turned up, drinking beer from a can that looked shockingly indecent on top of his iron-wrought, glass-topped desk with the onyx base and back. He was about six feet tall, had red hair, scarred, very masculine features, and eyes as blue as a spring sky.

He also had a crushing handshake and an outgoing personality. He brought two more cans of chilled beer from an exquisite sideboard, also of wrought-iron and thick glass, but with its interior obscured by a very delicate and lovely pastel brocade, slammed them on the desk and flung down two openers.

'Drink up, gentlemen,' he said. 'Don't give me that crap about cops not drinking an occasional beer on duty. I know better.'

Lieutenant Stokes declined. So did

Sam Adams but the powerful, compact man beyond the desk shook his head, grinning from ear to ear. 'Drink it, boys, or pull out. I take it personally when people won't drink with me.'

He meant it. That friendly big grin did not conceal the fact that Hale Ward meant everything he said. Now he sat, hunched and waiting, blue eyes bright with hard and candid antagonism.

Sam shrugged, took the can, opened it and took several swallows. Ward laughed. Lieutenant Stokes did likewise, and the tough hardness partially left Hale Ward's smile.

'Now let's get down to business,' he said, in command all the way. 'You're cops, and I've done something.'

'If you have,' said Sam, 'we haven't stumbled on to it yet. You have a lot of very expensive cloth here, in the shop.'

'Okay. What's behind that crack?'

'You are expecting another shipment. From the Orient. Twenty-four or twenty-five bolts of handmade silk and brocade.'

Hale Ward leaned forward and put aside his empty beer tin. He looked with frank interest from Stokes to Sam. 'You are correct. Two dozen bolts from a supplier in Hong Kong. Where do we go from there?'

'You have just hired a warehouse clerk.'

'I have just hired a book-keeper,' corrected Hale Ward. 'Herman Wales.'

Sam's eyes were ironic. 'Howard Wax, Herman Wales. He seems to be one of those who always use the same initials.'

Stokes nodded but Hale Ward didn't permit the lieutenant to speak, if indeed Lieutenant Stokes had intended to speak. 'I don't know any Howard Wax. As for my new book-keeper, he had very good references.'

'He always would have, Mister Ward,' said Stokes. 'If you'd advertised for a drape-hanger, I'll bet he'd have had references for that job too.'

Ward's alert blue gaze jumped back and forth. 'You're telling me I've hired a crook. Okay, now tell me just what the hell this guy can steal out of here? There is never more than maybe a couple of thousand dollars in cash around the store.

All our accounts are handled by cheque. If this bum would settle for chicken-feed, he could get the two thousand. Otherwise — does he specialize in glass desks like this damned thing here, or gold lamé draperies, or antique mosaic tile for vestibules — or what?'

'Oriental bolts of brocade and silk,' said Sam.

Ward threw up his arms. 'It's not even here. Are you saying this little nondescript guy knew in advance I'd be getting this stuff from Hong Kong?'

Sam looked at Lieutenant Stokes, looked back at Ward and said, 'Suppose you take a little drive with us, Mister Ward. I'll promise you one thing; of all the interesting afternoons you've spent in your life, this one should be the most completely astonishing.'

Hale Ward leaned and studied the faces of the two large men across the desk from him. He smiled and the smoky look returned to his eyes. 'Okay, boys, I'm game. I haven't always been an interior decorator. I've decorated a few *exteriors* too, in my time.' He turned slightly to tip an intercom key and say, 'Evelyn, I'll be out for the rest of the afternoon.' Without waiting for an acknowledgement he then rose, picked up the expensive sports jacket lying upon a small marble-topped table nearby and said, 'Let's go. We'll use my back exit.' He grinned broadly. 'It's the only way to go when you're playing cloak-and-dagger games.'

Sam was amused but Lieutenant Stokes seemed a little less than pleased at Hale Ward's treatment of what was, to him, a very serious matter.

20

Wait and See

After three hours at the detective bureaux, they took Hale Ward to dinner at a nearby cafe. He had been completely filled in, something the police seldom did with civilians, in fact there was an entire chapter in the Manual explaining why this was both inadvisable from the standpoint of security, and also why it usually only resulted in involvement with emotional people.

Hale Ward was not a particularly emotional person. Stokes and Sam Adams knew that before they'd ever met the man. As for security, it was Sam Adams's opinion that, the way events had transpired, the police were going to need outside help now, exactly as he'd anticipated them needing it right after the assassination of the wino named Charley, in the general hospital ward.

At dinner Hale Ward said that he would of course co-operate. He also said, with a whimsical look, that he had never imagined in his wildest hours that he could be involuntarily involved with a narcotics ring.

'It's like something out of a movie, except that in movies the smugglers use high-speed boats, moonless nights, stuff like that. These guys are really organized. Imagine, conning me with this little guy Herman Wales.'

'If it's any consolation,' said Stokes, 'you're not the first, Mister Ward. And nowadays when jobs are begging and people are hard to get, it's not so unusual that you should need a book-keeper.'

Hale Ward finished eating, lit a cigarette, tossed the pack on the table between his companions as though inviting them to help themselves, and ranged a bold gaze round the dining-room, which was moderately full of people he didn't know. 'If it all fits, gentlemen, I'll tell you one thing; I'm very impressed by the way this syndicate operates. My new book-keeper turns up the same day I get notification of the shipment of material from Hong Kong is to be air-freighted to me. *That* is organization.'

They had verified the air-freight route from Hong Kong an hour earlier, in Richard Stokes's office. They had also discussed the verifiable fact that using airfreight as a means of transporting their invisible contraband, being something the smugglers had not done before, perhaps was undertaken as the result of a rising demand for the narcotics.

'This thing,' mused Hale Ward, 'could run away with you. It could grow and grow.' He inhaled, exhaled, looked at Sam Adams and made a little grimace. 'I've seen addicts by the score in the Orient, and right here in New York City too. They make your skin crawl. If it were left to me I think I'd use the old Chinese system of punishing law-breakers.'

'How's that?'

Ward smiled very slightly. 'Well; you tell them to put their hands behind their backs. Then you tie their wrists tightly, then you ask them to kneel, which

251

they do, then you ask them to bend their heads forward as though praying — and you shoot them in the back of the head.' Ward threw up both hands. 'No more offences. Very thorough, very efficient. You are never bothered by second-offenders.'

Lieutenant Stokes reached for his coffee cup. 'We'll be entirely satisfied if you'll simply co-operate without shooting anyone, Mister Ward. All you have to do is call Sam's office the moment you get advance notice that cloth has arrived from Hong Kong, or, if the stuff arrives at the air-freight terminal the same day you're notified, you call us before sending for the shipment.'

'No problem,' replied the interior decorator. 'After we have the material, you set up the trap — right?'

'Right. With your co-operation.'

'You've got it, of course.'

Sam had an admonition. 'If you turn up at the store tomorrow looking or acting different in any way, don't think for a minute that new book-keeper of yours won't notice it. I'd say that after playing the part he's been playing for so long, nothing will get past their insideman.'

Ward wasn't worried. 'He won't get suspicious of me. If I had any doubts all I'd have to do would be out on a call all day.'

They finished eating, finished their after-dinner smoke, and drove Hale Ward back to within a block or so of his store, then promised to keep his place of business under surveillance, and left him to cruise on around where the sleek, black car still was parked out in front of the brownstone.

Stokes said, 'Let's call it a day. It all went off a lot better than I expected.'

Sam was a little tired, so when he nodded his head the movement was slightly sluggish. In the middle of the movement he suddenly stiffened. He had told Helen he'd take her to dinner tonight!

It was already close to ten o'clock, and although there would still be many places serving dinner, in all probability Helen was abed and asleep by now — grinding her teeth in unconscious wrath over being quite forgotten.

Stokes suddenly said, 'What's wrong? You look like something just fell on you.'

'I completely forgot a dinner-date with Helen.'

They were out front of the bureaux building by this time, and as Sam slowed at the kerbing for Lieutenant Stokes to alight, the officer said, 'That's certainly too bad, Sam. I hope she accepts your apology and explanation. Well, good night; see you first thing in the morning.'

Stokes walked away with a brisk step. Sam watched him disappear in the direction of his personal car, and scowled. It was all well and good for Richard Stokes to be only politely regretful, he didn't have to face Helen in the morning.

Sam drove on home, rummaged for cold-cuts in his refrigerator, drank a can of beer along with the improvised late snack while considering his predicament, and in the end decided to telephone Helen.

Her telephone rang seven times before she answered sounding only half awake. He said, 'Hi, Curly-head. I just got in. Listen; about that date we had — '

She slammed the telephone down at her end without uttering a single word.

Sam finished the cold-cuts, took the beer into the bathroom with him to be sipped while he stripped for a shower, and afterwards finished it with a towel draped round him as he took the can back to the tiny kitchenette for disposal.

A shower before bed always made Sam feel much better. It also he averred, made him sleep better. But tonight after he lay down, sleep would not come. He blamed that on the snack he'd eaten. He also blamed part of it on the feeling of guilt he had over inadvertently standing Helen up.

Then he slept.

By the time he left the flat the following morning it was almost eight o'clock. In order to sustain his long record of punctuality, he had to drive a bit fast, but he made it; he walked into the office with a couple of minutes to spare.

Helen neither raised her eyes nor interrupted her typing.

Sam considered her for a moment, stepped to the desk, leaned and pushed a big hand between roller and keyboard. Several keys hit his hand instead of the paper behind it, and Helen stopped typing, put both hands in her lap and looked up at him, smoky-eyed and hostile.

'You could have at least telephoned, Sam. There is absolutely no excuse for not even calling to say you would be tied up.'

'The truth was, I forgot.'

'Thanks a lot. I'm flattered no end that I'm so important to you.'

'That's got nothing to do with it, Curly-head.'

'Stop calling me that. My name is Helen.'

'That's got nothing to do with it, Helen. Lieutenant Stokes and I worked out a way to trap Borzoi, his entire crew, and grab a big shipment of that impregnated cloth. We were with a man named Hale Ward until only a short while before I called you last night, setting things up.'

'And you couldn't have taken two minutes to — '

'Helen, believe me, if I'd remembered, I'd have done it.' Sam eased down upon the desk, took a limp hand and held it. 'You know how much the Ludwig-Borzoi thing means to us all. We're within hours of concluding it. Isn't that a mitigating condition?'

The telephone rang. Helen gave a little start, jerked her hand from Sam's grip and reached for the thing before it could jangle again.

The caller was Lieutenant Stokes. Helen passed the telephone to Sam, who rose off the desk and said his name, then waited. Stokes didn't make him wait long.

'I've put a surveillance team on Ward's store. I've also detailed a man to keep an eye on Howard Wax — née Herman Wales — and I'm calling now to ask whether you'd prefer watching the brownstone personally, or whether you'd just as soon keep yourself free and have me put someone else on that job?'

'Someone else,' said Sam. 'Has Ward called yet this morning?'

'He hasn't called me. Now I take it he hasn't contacted you either. Well; it may be a bit early.'

'That air-freight shipment should arrive this morning, though. Lieutenant, it may not be a bad idea to have someone go out to the terminal, pick up the schedule and stay right with it all the way through to Ward's store. I have no idea at all that Borzoi would attempt a hi-jacking between the terminal and the store, but I'm satisfied that if anything made him suspicious, that's exactly what he'd do. A quarter of a million dollars worth of heroin means an awful lot of money.'

Stokes concurred, saying he'd send a man out to keep an eye on the air-freight from Hong Kong as soon as it arrived. He then rang off and Helen, who'd been candidly eavesdropping, spoke to Sam as though they hadn't been having an argument moments earlier, as though he hadn't neglected her shamefully and she hadn't been sizzling-mad over that.

'Are you absolutely certain this Hale Ward is dependable, Sam? Suppose he decides, after thinking it all over, to sell out to Robert Borzoi. He could, you know; Borzoi would pay cash and undoubtedly a great amount of it, to be warned that the police are closing in. Sam; by now he could perhaps be half way back to the Orient. Airplanes fly all night, you know.'

Sam smiled. 'So they do, Curly-head. But I'm satisfied about Hale Ward.' He leaned and quickly pecked her on the cheek. 'Lunch, a little later?'

'Not on you life, you great horse. You'll be skulking round a store somewhere and forget it's lunchtime, or you'll be supervising a surround somewhere, and here I'll be sitting. Mister Garfunckel wouldn't do a thing like that to Margery.'

Sam agreed. 'A guy with a name like Garfunckel wouldn't dare,' he said, and didn't explain what he meant as he turned to go out into the corridor. 'I'll be in Lieutenant Stokes's dive if you want me.'

'I think he's replacing me in your

259

affections, Sam. Are you aware that Lieutenant Stokes is married?'

'Very funny,' he growled, and left the office.

Helen sighed, rose, went over and closed the door after him, returned to her desk and with a little resigned shake of the head, resumed her typing.

It was by then almost eleven o'clock.

Sam entered Stokes's office just as the telephone on Miss Fein's desk rang. The lieutenant's head appeared round the nearby doorway, and Sam also stopped in his tracks, staring. Miss Fein briskly plucked the instrument from its cradle, spoke, listened a moment, then raised her eyes to the two stern detectives with colour mounting into her cheeks, and shook her head.

She said, 'Please . . . call back this afternoon. Look; we can't have the telephone tied up this morning.' As she put the telephone back on its little stand she smiled weakly.

Sam looked at Lieutenant Stokes. 'Garfunckel,' he said.

Stokes looked down his nose at Miss

Fein. She nodded back, red and flustered, then began working very industriously at her typewriter as Sam passed on by, into Stokes's private office.

'Nothing yet, I take it,' said Sam, and the lieutenant, still looking annoyed, shook his head.

'Nothing yet. We've got four under-cover men out, with instructions to report at once if anything breaks, and who do we get?'

'Garfunckel,' muttered Sam, fishing in a pocket for his smokes. 'Don't worry; Ward will co-operate.'

'I'm not worried about that,' said Stokes. 'I'm worried about a foul-up; something happening that'll spill the beans.'

Sam lit up, took a chair across from his superior, and nodded. He had the identical anxiety, but in him it just wasn't as near the surface as it was in Lieutenant Stokes.

21

Strategy

The call came at eleven-thirty, only a half hour before the lunch-hour rush. The air-freight had arrived and Lieutenant Stokes's man at the terminal was calling to report that a common carrier had tossed it into his lorry along with quite a large number of other parcels which had arrived on the same flight. The undercover detective had the van in sight, and would proceed now to follow it.

Stokes relayed this information to Sam and they both hastened down to Sam's car for the drive to Ward's interior decorating shop, after the lieutenant had called ahead alerting Hale Ward.

They discussed procedures on the way. As Sam said, in the first place there was very little chance that deliveryman would bring Hale Ward's consignment along first. And secondly, Howard Wax-Herman Wales would not realise the shipment from Hong Kong had arrived, in all probability, until it arrived at the store. Of course he would then alert Robert Borzoi and without much doubt, the stateside narcotics establishment would move at once to burglarize Hale Ward's shop.

'We can organize to pick them up one at a time, or we can nab Borzoi and Wax alone, and take the other four in their hideout at the brownstone,' said Sam. 'But in my view — not entirely from the standpoint of personal gratification although that sure as hell is involved — I'd like to catch the lot of them in Ward's backroom, in the act of stealing that Hong Kong shipment.'

Stokes agreed. 'Best way, no doubt of it.'

Hale Ward was outside when they arrived. He climbed into Sam's car without a word and pointed towards a lunchroom down the street. 'Running a risk of Wales seeing us together,' he said, 'when he goes out to lunch. We'd better go down to that restaurant ahead; it's very exclusive and very expensive; no chance of Wales showing up.'

They found Ward's words to be very true, for not only was the place very expensive, it was also, despite the noon rush-hour, only about half full.

Ward guided them to a gloomy table far back. He'd been notified by telephone, he said, that a shipment of cloth addressed to him would be delivered that afternoon.

The informant had been the office of the delivery company whose van had picked up the goods. An outfit that did almost all Hale Ward's pick-up and delivery work.

Ward said, 'And this will be it, eh?'

Stokes nodded. 'I thought we'd possibly have a day or two. Not that it matters. The sooner we conclude things the better. Mister Ward . . . '

The red-headed man spread his hands. 'Nothing to worry about, Lieutenant. I'll see that my office-girl carries on as usual. I'll have Mister Wales check in the goods and put them away in the backroom, and I'll look at the tally with him, in order to be sure it's all right to pay the delivery charges, then I'll go back to my office. Okay?'

Sam smiled at Ward, thinking it was fortunate that this time they'd got a person they could safely involve. Stokes looked at Sam. The lieutenant had kept his word about not taking-over Sam's case. He was keeping it now as well.

Sam said after they'd got all the arrangements made, they would notify Ward by telephone. He also suggested that Mister Ward go home a bit early this evening.

Ward began to frown at Sam. 'What does that mean? Sounds like a hint for me not to show up for the fireworks.'

Sam nodded. 'Exactly. It's not that we have any doubts about your ability to take whatever comes along. It's simply that we can't allow civilians to get involved. Those are old, established Department rules.'

'Wait a minute,' snapped Hale Ward, that tough, hard look returning to his face in a rush. 'Whose store is this, these monkeys are trying to use; whose business is involved? Boys, I couldn't care less what your Department rules are — I'll be back here tonight.'

'You could tip them off just by coming back when Wales knows by now that you don't do that.'

'But I do come back. Every now and then I return to the office to work on designs and arrangements. Ask Evelyn. Wales hasn't been here long enough to know, but the office-girl has. And if Wales got nosy, she'd tell him I occasionally come back after hours.'

Lieutenant Stokes was adamant. 'We appreciate your personal interest, but if you come back you're not only running a hell of a good chance of getting shot, but you're also very likely to louse up *our* arrangements. Mister Ward, please don't do it.'

For a few moments the three of them sat, exchanging looks, then Sam used the final alternative. 'Look, Mister Ward; just tell us you are, or you are not, going to return to the store tonight?'

Something in those words rang a little alarm-bell in Ward's mind. He scowled and said, 'Why? What happens if I answer affirmatively?'

Sam smiled. 'Then I'm going to arrest you on the spot, take you and book you for interfering with policemen in the performance of their duty. You can have a lawyer spring you in a half hour.'

'And I would, don't you ever think otherwise!'

'Okay. And I'll have a detective waiting just outside the doors of the building to re-arrest you on the grounds of — '

'Hold it,' said Ward, leaning back. 'I get the message.' He shook his head at Sam. 'All right, you win. I'll go back now and hang around until the shipment arrives, then call you. Afterwards, I'll check it in, then I'll leave for the day.' He nodded. 'Good luck. I'll see you in the morning, eh?'

Stokes smiled. 'We appreciate this kind of co-operation, believe me.'

Ward arose looking slightly pithy, nodded and walked away. Over at the cashier's counter he dropped a green note on the glass counter, jerked a thumb towards the two large men still eating, and walked out of the restaurant.

Stokes said, 'For a minute there I thought you'd be called on to make good that threat, Sam.'

They departed from the restaurant ten minutes later, drove over to view the brownstone, saw Borzoi's car still parked where it had been the day before, then made one more pass out front of the interior decorating shop before heading bee-line straight back to the bureaux-building.

In Lieutenant Stokes's office they co-ordinated their efforts. First, they pulled every plain clothes observer out of the area except one. That was the man stationed to watch Ward's shop. Secondly, the moment that detective called in who had been keeping the delivery lorry under surveillance, they told him to make a discreet study of Ward's building, front and rear, then bring in his sketch of the place showing every means of access burglars would use.

Finally, they got a city map for the neighbourhood and spread it atop Stokes's desk to plan their strategy of sealing off the store and every route leading in, or out, of the immediate vicinity.

It was two o'clock before the detective who'd been following the delivery van walked into Stokes's office. He had a chart of the area and a smaller, more detailed drawing of Ward's store.

Unless the burglars used the front entrance, they would have access to the building from a steel-jacketed rear door which led directly into the rear storeroom, where the Hong Kong shipment would be kept. There was one rear window, barred against burglary with thick steel. Evidently some former inhabitant of the building had either taken precautions against burglary, or else the place had been armoured like that during the process of construction, but whichever it was, as Sam said, while it wouldn't be impossible to break in from the rear, it would take a lot of time and muscle to do it.

There was a sky-light in the roof which offered access. But that was of course locked, and access to it was by an exposed fire-ladder up the south side of the building.

'Exposed,' said the detective who'd made the drawing. 'But if they don't hit the place until maybe one or two in the morning, it's doubtful that anyone would be abroad to see them.'

Sam said, pointing to the sketch. 'Front door. Wales has had a couple of days to get keys made to the doors, front and rear. Maybe he couldn't borrow the original keys, but you can depend on the fact that he's had opportunities to make wax impressions. My guess is that he'll use the front door to let them in.' Sam bent to study the sketch. 'How wide is that back alley?' he asked the detective who'd made the sketch. 'Wide enough for a parked car to block it?'

'Yeah. It's only a delivery-way. You can block it at both ends easy.'

Stokes beamed. 'Back door, Sam. No one would see them back there.'

Sam nodded. 'I still like the front door,' he exclaimed. 'Borzoi is no fool. He won't put his car in back where someone could block it. I like the front door.'

'But the damned car will be in plain sight out there,' protested Stokes, pointing to the broad avenue with which they were both familiar.

Sam didn't argue. It wasn't that important an issue. He said, 'All right, Lieutenant. We'll use four prowl-cars; two to seal off that back alley at both ends, and each car to have a team armed with rifles and shotguns. The other two cars we'll station a block or so away around front, out of sight on side-streets, to block that route off too, in front and behind, Borzoi's car.' Sam looked up. Lieutenant Stokes was nodding his head and studying the sketch.

Sam then said. 'You and I will get into position directly across from Ward's shop. Also, just in case something goes wrong, we'll have some men inside the brownstone. I don't think Borzoi and his crew will get back there, but while those officers are staking the place out, they can also begin rounding up all that equipment used to re-claim the heroin.

271

We'll need it for evidence in any case.'

The detective who'd made the drawing said, 'Lieutenant, what about the back?'

Sam had the answer to that. 'Four men to cover the alleyway from roofs back there.'

The detective nodded, looking satisfied, and the telephone rang. It was Hale Ward. He reported crisply that he had just finished checking-in the Hong Kong shipment with his book-keeper. He also said, 'That guy's as cool as a cucumber. He couldn't have acted less interested if it had been a genuine shipment of stuff . . . Are you guys all set up?'

Stokes said, 'Yes. We've just finished planning the trap. You take care of your end; make sure the girl goes home, and you do the same.'

Ward said, 'I'm handy in a scrap.'

The lieutenant declined the implied offer, rang off and looked at Sam. 'Well? Ward reports his new employee helped him check-in the cloth. The only thing that can louse us up, would be if Borzoi decides not to hit the store tonight.'

Sam had a cryptic answer to that.

'He'll hit it. In fact, by now the book-keeper has undoubtedly found a way to telephone Borzoi at the brownstone, and Borzoi won't hesitate for a very good reason: Franz Ludwig tore a piece off a bolt of brocade. Borzoi won't take a chance on that happening again. Suppose Hale Ward decided tomorrow to sell a bolt of brocade, or even half a bolt . . . ?' Sam smiled and Lieutenant Stokes smiled back, a bit thinly, as he spoke.

'That could be the most expensive bit of cloth in New York.'

Sam wanted to cruise back to the neighbourhood for one long last look around. He told Stokes he'd be back later, unless something came up that would require his presence, in which case he'd call in.

Stokes was agreeable.

Sam went first to his office where Helen was waiting, full of questions. He explained what was in progress and she promptly began worrying.

'Sam, why don't you just surround the entire area with men and close in without waiting for nightfall? It's too dangerous, the way you are planning it. If you corner those men in the back room of that store, they'll fight. You know they will.'

Sam leaned, brushed his lips over her cheek and stepped back. 'You do the worrying, I'll do the arresting. By the way, if anyone wants me you know how to make contact. I'll have my Department car.'

He went to the door, felt sorry for her and said, 'Curly-head; tomorrow night a big dinner at the English place. To celebrate. Okay?'

'If you're not in hospital, Sam Adams. You be careful!'

He agreed, walked out, and actually remembered to close the door.

22

After Dark

By five o'clock the boulevard where Hale Ward's shop was located had been very discreetly staked out by four unmarked police cars, each with a crew of two men in it. By Lieutenant Stokes's orders each team had shot-guns, rifles, and two-way radios, plus their usual side-arms.

Sam probably could have obtained permission from the owner of the building directly across from Ward's store to establish a command-post on the roof, but he did not make the effort.

A handy fire-escape ladder gave access. From up there he contacted one of the unmarked police cars to ask the officer who took his call to put in a call to Lieutenant Stokes over the regular police-band, advising Stokes where Sam was, and saying that Stokes should meet him on the roof.

After that call had been transmitted, Sam used his two-way radio to contact the plain clothes man who had Borzoi's car and residence under surveillance.

'They probably won't move until well after nightfall, but you keep close watch, and the moment they come out and get into the car, call me. Don't delay!'

He lit a cigarette, tried to get comfortable in an area where personal comfort had never entered anyone's mind, and occasionally leaned to watch the store.

He saw that beautiful office-girl depart. She left a little before six, and up until she departed Sam was worrying about her. After that he waited for Wales to depart, and that didn't happen until after six o'clock.

Sam watched the book-keeper amble northward along the boulevard mingling easily with the crowd of other local employees, and had to admit that Wax-Wales, or whatever his name was, couldn't have been improved on, if someone needed a thoroughly nondescript individual. He even dressed in a mousy way.

There were a few store lights coming on up and down the boulevard by the time Lieutenant Stokes scaled the rear-wall ladder and panted his way across the rooftop to join Sam. His first words touched a raw nerve with Sam.

'Are they all gone?'

Sam swore. 'That damned Hale Ward is still in there. I thought he told us he'd fake a business call and be out of the store this afternoon.'

'He did.'

'Do you see that blue El Dorado Cadillac in the parking area?'

Stokes looked and grunted something indistinguishable under his breath, but as he started to pull back a man came out of the shop, locked the front door and without so much as a glance around, hiked directly to the blue Cadillac and drove off.

Sam shook his head as he and Stokes watched the car head briskly northward up the wide, crowded boulevard. 'I've got some doubts about Hale Ward.'

Stokes was startled. 'You mean — you think he might be involved, Sam?'

'No. Not that. I've just got a doubt that he's going to keep out of this.'

But the blue car did not return, at least Sam didn't see it again as he settled to his vigil. Now and then Lieutenant Stokes contacted the waiting police teams. He also contacted the man watching Borzoi's car. Time ran on, the traffic got steadily lighter down there in the boulevard, and after ten o'clock when Sam rose to stretch, and mention that there was a chill creeping into the air, Stokes merely glanced at his wrist and yawned.

It was one o'clock when the man watching the brown-stone called. 'Five men came out of the house and are now getting into the car.'

Sam repeated that for the benefit of Lieutenant Stokes, then he said, 'Stay over there. When the other officers move in to ransack the house, go over and lend them a hand. Which way is Borzoi's car moving?'

'Northward. Now it's turning westward into a side-street heading towards the boulevard.'

'Sign off,' ordered Sam, briskly. 'Go

278

and help the other officers.' He put aside the two-way radio, glanced at his watch, turned and stiffly waited for a sleek dark car to emerge on to the boulevard. It did, but not for so long that Sam was beginning to fidget.

Stokes picked up the two-way Sam had put aside, called the waiting cars alerting them. He also warned the men stationed on the roof over behind Ward's store. His orders were crisp and clear.

'Do nothing until I tell you. Then close in on the alley, blocking it off at both ends. Stay behind your cars. If they make a break for it they'll have guns. You men in front stand ready. I have a bull-horn. The minute they come into my sight with the bolts of cloth I'm going to jump them. Be ready.'

The sleek car cruised past Hale Ward's store, went as far as the alley entrance and turned in. Stokes said he'd been sure they'd use that back alley. But the car backed clear, only utilising that open space to make a turn, then came cruising back, slower still, towards the front of the store.

It stopped and for a full minute no one alighted. Sam leaned towards Stokes. 'They're careful.' Stokes nodded without taking his eyes off the car far below, or uttering a sound.

A tallish man finally left the car, walked briskly to the recessed front door of Ward's shop, was lost there briefly in darkness, then turned and gestured. Evidently he'd unlocked the door. At once four other men piled out of the car and swiftly crossed over into the darkness by the door.

Sam let off a big, shaky breath, looked at his watch and said, 'Lieutenant, time to close the trap.'

Stokes put the two-way radio to his face. 'Move in; you men out back seal off that alley and watch closely now. They may have a key to the rear door and try to escape that way when I hail them. You boys on the roof over there — shoot only if they fire first. You men in the side-streets, keep your motors running. The minute you hear my bull-horn drive midway out into the boulevard and get on the far side of your cars.'

Stokes looked at Sam as though under the impression he might have neglected something. He hadn't. Sam smiled and stepped up closer to the low parapet around their rooftop vantage point. 'They ought to be coming out soon now.' Sam drew his service revolver but Stokes simply kept the intercom radio to his face, watching the building with a strong and unmoving stare.

The smugglers had been inside about ten minutes and Sam could feel Lieutenant Stokes beginning to move uneasily beside him, when that same lean, tallish man appeared, unburdened. He strolled to the car, glancing quickly left and right, then, evidently satisfied, he turned and raised his arm to signal.

That was when Lieutenant Stokes picked up the bull-horn.

'You men in front of that store freeze right where you are. This is the police!'

The bull-horn made Stokes's voice sound as though it were coming from an old time gramophone, but the words, enunciated clearly, were distinct and loud in the late-night hush.

There was another sound as two patrol cars suddenly shot out of side-streets north and south, braked to squealing halts broadsides in the empty roadway, and doors slammed.

Stokes called again. It seemed that the little crowd of men down there, four of them weighted down with bolts of cloth, were dumbstruck.

'Don't move! You are surrounded and under police guns. Stand perfectly still!'

One man cried out, dropped his cloth and fled up the northward sidewalk. A rifle picked him up fifty feet from his friends and dropped him in the gutter. That single muzzleblast made a frightful sound. Echoes were still slamming back and forth off store-fronts when Stokes spoke again.

'Borzoi, tell the others not to try it. They don't have a chance!'

The tallish man beside the car turned, his face a pale blue, as he finally located where Stokes was calling from. Slowly Borzoi turned back. Sam heard him say something to his three remaining confederates but the distance was too great for the words to be distinguishable.

Stokes used the bull-horn again. 'Put the cloth down. Put your hands on top of your heads. Walk to the edge of the kerbing and stand perfectly still there. Stay away from the car. Borzoi; move off. Get away from the car!'

Lieutenant Stokes had the initiative. Doubtless the trapped men considered fighting back, but they could see their companion lying sprawled in the gutter. He was a very strong incentive for them to do exactly as they were told.

Stokes, no novice at his kind of thing, kept the initiative. He got them moving towards the kerbing as Sam Adams picked up the two-way radio and ordered the teams in from north and south, warning them to be extremely careful. He then put aside the radio, turned and trotted to the edge of the roof and started down the fire-escape, two rungs at a time.

Borzoi and his companions were lined up on the kerbing, hands on their heads. Four plain clothes detectives were edging up the sidewalk towards them, from behind. These men had their guns up and ready.

Whatever chance the smugglers had ever possessed they had let it go by. Now, it would be suicide for any of them to make a break for it.

Stokes kept haranguing them, holding their attention. Sam came from around the building across the way and stepped forth into plain sight of the men along the opposite kerbing. He too had his service revolver at the ready.

He crossed the street with four sets of glazed eyes upon him. Where he stopped, ten feet away, facing the prisoners, he spoke to them for the first time.

'Four policemen will frisk you from behind. Make a move of any kind and I'll drop you where you stand.'

The plain clothes men moved in to run experienced hands over the captives. They took a weapon from each man, then stepped back several feet. Sam eased the hammer down on his revolver, shoved it into the belt-holster beneath his coat and stepped up in front of the tallish, lean man. 'Borzoi?'

'Yes.'

'You are under arrest for the murder of Franz Ludwig.'

The black-olive eyes widened on Sam. 'Who?'

Sam said, 'Sauerkraut. Does that sound more familiar? And for another wino; a man called Charley who was shot with a silencer in the hospital drunk-tank. Two murders, Borzoi.'

The pale, rather handsome youthful face with its black eyes, black straight hair and flat, high cheekbones, tensed slightly. Sam shook his head. 'Don't try it, Borzoi. You couldn't get past me, let alone the rifles aimed at you.'

Lieutenant Stokes came walking up, still clutching the bull-horn. He motioned for the four detectives standing behind the captives to come closer. 'Cuff them,' he said. Then he turned, as Sam was also doing, and studied the face of each captive.

Sam walked fifty feet away and knelt to look at the man in the gutter. He was dead. That one bullet had caught him high in the chest and dead-centre.

It was good shooting for a moving target on a dark night. Sam went back where the captives were at long last beginning to relax.

Other policemen were coming out of the alley at both ends. Sam jerked his head at Stokes, they went over by the front door of Hale Ward's shop and bent to examine the helter-skelter bolts of silk and brocade. Sam touched a corner of cloth to his lips, then spat. The taste was like bitter almonds compounded with salt.

A policeman called out as a large car came cruising up. Sam and Lieutenant Stokes turned in time to recognize Ward's car. Sam grunted and gave his head a wry shake. 'I told you I had my doubts about him.'

Ward climbed out tieless and hatless, grinning from ear to ear as he reached in and bodily dragged someone else out of the car. When Sam and Stokes got over there they recognized the man known down at the Asche and Cohn warehouse as Howard Wax, and known to Hale Ward as Herman Wales.

Ward said triumphantly, 'I picked him up at his flat and brought him along.'

Sam groaned. Wales-Wax could say he'd been kidnapped. Sam was about to say something unpleasant to Ward when the visibly shaken book-keeper turned to Stokes with a high-pitched bleat.

'Look officer; you guarantee me protection and I'll tell you plenty.'

Robert Borzoi, being led past handcuffed, heard that and turned in mid-stride, hissing a curse. The officer who had Borzoi in hand gave the prisoner a rough tug and a rougher push.

'Keep movin', you, or I'll carry you!'

Stokes accepted the cigarette Sam offered. He said, 'Mister Wales — or Wax — whatever your name is, I think I can promise you protection. But I've got to tell you that anything you say now can be used in evidence against you, and that before you say a word you are entitled to have your attorney with you.'

The slight, worried man bobbed his head up and down all the time Lieutenant Stokes was speaking. He evidently knew all this. Then he said, 'I know what a narcotics rap means. I'll co-operate in exchange for consideration. Okay?'

Stokes nodded. 'Okay.'

Sam Adams turned and walked over to a telephone kiosk on the opposite side of the road, dialled a number and when a somewhat breathless voice answered after the second ring, he said, 'Curly-head, you can go to bed now. It went off as smooth as — silk. See you in the morning. We can start preparing the reports and racking up the evidence. And then there'll be dinner tomorrow night. Okay?'

'Sam . . . I could cry. Okay. You are all right?'

'Hungry that's all. I've been on a damned rooftop since before sundown.'

'Sam; can you get away from there?'

'Yes. It's all over but taking them in and booking them. They don't need me for that.'

'You come right over here. I'll have a big dinner ready.'

'Curly-head, do you know what *time* it is?'

'Of course I know what time it is.

Don't you think I've been sitting here watching the clock? Come right over.'

'The neighbours will talk.'

'They're in bed. And to hell with them anyway. Are you coming?'

'I'll be there in fifteen minutes, Curly-head.'

THE END